MORDEC'S QUEST

THE THRILLING ADVENTURES OF MORDEC THE VIKING

Mordec Raids England
Mordec's Quest
Mordec and the Hidden Hand
Mordec and the Lost Boys
Mordec the Conqueror

THE THRILLING ADVENTURES OF
MORDEC THE VIKING

BOOK 2

MORDEC'S QUEST

JILLIAN BECKER

Typesetting and Cover Design by
FormattingExperts.com

Published by Gothenburg Books
ISBN 978-1-7327275-2-6

contents

Mordec's Quest

To my grandchildren:
Matthew & Aaron Slipper
Jessica & Elizabeth Dilworth
Sam & Charlotte Westrop

the troll

The snow lay deep on the Northlands. Icicles hung from rocks, trees, roofs and beams. When a door opened and a face peered out, all that the little eyes in it could see was an armoury of thick round white swords and daggers made by the three dumb smiths of winter: the wet, the cold, and the lintel. The face looked out because it was morning, though there was nothing to tell a creature that day had come or noon was near except the inner clock of habit. If a body had slept for so many hours it must wake and work for a stretch, and that stretch must or might be day.

'Grrr!' the creature growled, baring his few teeth. He went back in to fetch an axe from his wall and with it he chopped away the white blades. When he could see what there was to see of the snowbound land he rested on his axe, and scanning the low horizon and the rise of a small hill he muttered 'Will he come now? Surely he will come!'

Though known as The Troll because he was strangely shaped, with a head sunk like a stopper in a drum of a body, and stumpy limbs, and fingers as gnarled and hairy as roots, he was no more and no less than human. Clucking his annoyance or disappointment, he was beginning to withdraw his head with its crop of black hair back into the smoky dimness of his house, built under the mountain behind him, so that he could slam his door on the cold emptiness of the world, when his small deep-set eyes were held by a movement. Was that not something appearing on the opposite snowhill, darker against the dark sky? It was.

'It is he. Must be. Who else? So he has come. Now we shall know.'

A figure grew on the rounded top of the low hill. There it stopped still, a black triangle on a black block.

'Arrgh! Let him stare and hesitate, and then let him come and knock. I'll not stand here and freeze while he makes up his mind.' The Troll stepped back inside and shut his door. But he waited just behind it breathing the smell of the warm spiced wine he had drunk for breakfast up to his own lumpy nose from a protruding lower lip. Then he chuckled, and his little eyes glittered. 'He'll come. He'll knock. Even if he's scared. Noseyness will bring him. It's brought him this far and it'll bring him all the way. Everyone's just as nosey as I am.'

The figure on the hill was not a man but a boy, already as tall as many a fullgrown man. He was hooded and cloaked and booted and mittened in wolf's fur, his boots tied on criss-cross with cowhide thongs, his face greased blackly in patches with lard and soot against the cold.

He stood looking towards the door where he had seen the dwarfish fellow appear and disappear. But he was not hesitating out of fear. He was considering the oddities he saw. Not just the fellow who'd now gone in and slammed the door—his oddness was no more than he'd been led to expect—but the house! It was too small to be a dwelling place. No more than a hut, a hovel, a shed of rough logs. And folk said that The Troll was rolling in luxury, that he lived in a grand palace under the mountain, its halls stuffed with treasures stolen by sorcery from the rich men and princes of the South and East.

But perhaps, the boy thought, he wasn't seeing well enough in this dim light. He drew a pair of eyeglasses from the top of a boot and put them on. He'd removed them when ice had begun to film them over. Now, wiped clean, they showed him that the hut was small indeed, sunk into the side of the mountain like The Troll's own head into his body.

The boy had never ventured here before. It had taken him three hours trudging, after he'd got out of the sleigh of Hrut the Pedlar. 'Keep the forest on your right and when you get to the end of it you'll see Trollshill ahead of you,' Hrut had directed him.

Now here he was with his toes aching and his nose numb, wondering whether he would be welcome and warmed in that miserable little hut, or turned into a wolf, a worm, or an idiot by magic spells.

But he'd been summoned to fetch a letter and his curiosity was strong. Who could have written it? Someone in England perhaps? And how had it been borne over the sea in winter? So unlikely was the news of its arrival that when Hrut's daft daughter

Thorgerd had come to the door and shouted 'Letter, letter,' as she'd been told to, he'd thought at first that she was merely babbling. Then she'd become more insistent. 'For you, for you, for the honey blue boy.'

That was her name for him, 'honey blue boy', because his father sold honey and his clothes were blue. He'd smiled then and said 'A letter for me?' 'Letter, letter,' she'd repeated, nodding, glad to be understood, and then pointing to her father's sleigh which waited beyond the orchard gate.

Hrut had been entrusted with the message a week ago, he said, when last he'd been at The Troll's before these latest blizzards, but only now in the weather's lull had judged it safe enough to harness the dogs and drive to Hauk's orchard.

'Come, come, come,' Thorgerd had urged the boy impatiently as he'd put on furs for the journey. And as they'd sat in the sleigh under bearskins, she'd held his hand tightly with both of hers, and now and then she'd kissed his face. She was happy to be in his company, happier still when he smiled at her. But the boy had been full of uncertainty about what lay ahead. He reasoned that if Hrut visited The Troll and was never harmed, he too could go there. But what of Thorgerd? Was she daft because of The Troll's wickedness? Had he cast a spell on her? Reason soothed him again. Hrut wouldn't trade with The Troll if he blamed him for his daughter's plight.

'Anyway,' he thought, 'I've come this far, and I want the letter.'

Resolutely he descended the snowslope and knocked loudly to show he wasn't afraid. The door opened at once and small deep-set eyes looked up at him, darting and suspicious.

'Yes? Who are you? What do you want?' The Troll asked in a high, quavering voice.

'I am Mordec son of Hauk,' the boy replied boldly. 'Thorgerd the Daft came to my house and told me you have a letter that was sent to me.'

'Mordec hmm? A strange name you have, boy. Outlandish. I don't like anything that is strange and outlandish. A person doesn't know where he is with it. But let me think. Why yes, I do have a letter for you. Well, come on, come in! Odds-bods, I can't keep m'door open all of a winter's day.'

Mordec stepped into a narrow, smoky space. Two or three rushlights flickering against the walls illuminated little beyond themselves.

'This way,' The Troll said in a changed voice, deep now and perfectly steady, as he flung open a pair of doors at the back of the hut. Then Mordec saw that the hut itself was only a short entrance leading to a large hall dug out of the mountain. So at least some of the stories he'd heard were true. The Troll did live in an underground palace, and it was full of treasures. Many lively torches lit up marble statues, tapestries, silver shields and jewelled swords, piles of thong-tied or string-stitched bales, and barrels and boxes bound with iron or studded with nails.

'This way,' The Troll said again, opening another pair of double doors solid and varnished, their handles made of twisted bronze. On outward-turning awkward feet he padded, leading the boy into a hall yet more vast, more splendid. Here were tables laden with platters and vessels of gold and silver, bronze and glass. They held dead feathered fowls, a baked boar's head, and piles of fruits. Fruits of the summer! These seemed to prove, Mordec thought, that magic really was worked inside this mountain.

In the middle of the room The Troll turned to face his visitor. 'Mordec, eh?' he said, and his mouth with its protruding lower lip curled up at the comers in a smile of sorts, revealing a few teeth and the gaps between them. He stood with his feet planted wide apart as he regarded Mordec. He put his head on one side, screwed up one eye and said, 'You needn't be afraid of me, y'know. I'll not harm you.'

'Good—then *I'll* not harm *you*,' Mordec said in a tone even firmer than The Troll's.

'You can take off your furs. It's warm in here. The cold is never let in.'

Warm it was. Mordec began to unwrap himself. The Troll clapped his hands and a tall, gaunt, yellow-haired woman, neither young nor old, dressed in a garment that would seem to have been made out of a multitude of long green leaves, came in through a side-door and held out her hands to take the boy's cloak and mittens and boots away.

'That's right, give your wet things to Roxane and she will dry them for you. Now rest.' A dark, knobby, hairy finger with a long, curved, horny nail, pointed to a couch draped in scarlet silk and Mordec sat on it. The Troll climbed into a huge chair, sat with his bandy legs crossed under him and folded his arms.

'My name is Julius,' he said harshly. But his tone softened and became quite lyrical as he went on. 'It was not the name my parents gave me. I chose it. I named myself after Julius Caesar, if you know who he was. My parents took one look at me and decided I wasn't worth naming. They'd have kept me chained to a barrel like a dog and fed me on scraps if I hadn't started talking early—and very persuasively. That proved to them I was human. Later when I picked up reading writing and reckoning faster than a jarl's son, they named me, not after my father and grandfather but after a stranger who'd passed through the village once and had been ugly like me, as they explained to me. Hans his name was, and that's what they called me, and they began to coddle me decently, keeping me out of sight of other folk, but thinking they might turn me to some use after all. But before I go on, tell me this. Are you thirsty? Hungry? Will you drink spiced wine? Will you eat aurochs, or ptarmigan, or dog?'

'I've only a few small coins my father gave me to pay for the letter, not for meat and wine.'

'I'll take payment for the letter, but I'd give you wine as I would any friend who comes into my house. Listen! When I was a nameless child I schemed and planned to become two things that none who saw me then would expect me ever to become: rich and useful. Useful and rich can be the same thing, I thought. How does a person become rich? He can loot and steal but he might not live long to enjoy his riches.

But if you provide what others want—ah-hah! So I made up my mind to become a provider of things that folk want. And when I grew up—in a manner of speaking, that is, because as you can see I didn't grow *up* very much, more *out*—that's what I became. And am. A trader. Not a trader who travels about with goods and guards, but who stores what others fetch and carry. You see, I play a part in the world without moving much about in it.'

Mordec looked round and asked, 'The grapes, peaches, plums—where do they come from in this season?'

Either Julius didn't hear or he chose not to answer. He went on: 'All goods come to me. Does the world contain a commodity I do not have a sample of, a store of, sometimes even all of? To me come all things grown, gathered, fattened, fangled, and from here go forth again. In a sense, I'm at the center of the world. All paths lead to me, while I seldom venture beyond my own walls. Now you, I suppose, want to sail the seas and fight battles?'

'Sail the seas, yes. I want to see other lands.'

'What is your father?'

'A beekeeper and meadmaker.'

'And that's not good enough for you?'

'I want to learn about—'

'Yes? About what?'

'Whatever I can. I want to find out what's going on and—'

'And?'

'Learn things.'

'From books?'

'People and books.'

'And I thought *I* was nosey! But tell me, how will you earn your keep if you spend your life nosing into things?'

'A man who knows a lot is stronger than others. Without having armies and gold.'

'You mean you want to be a wizard?'

'I'm not sure what I mean. But first I want to see the world.'

'Well that's usual enough among your folk. And you can't have seen much of it yet.'

'I was in England last summer.'

'England, eh? What a boast! And so—what did you learn there? What did you see?'

'I saw inside an Earl's castle.'

'And?'

'And knights jousting.'

'And?'

'And a horse race.'

'And?'

'I was tried for a crime I hadn't done and I was sentenced to death and only saved at the last moment.'

'Hmmm. That's a big thing to happen to a boy. I'd have thought it would be enough. You want more? You want the world to knock you on the head again?'

Mordec stood up. 'My letter—will you give it to me now?'.

'I will.'

'Can you tell me where it came from and how it came?'

'Where it started from I couldn't say. It got here before these recent blizzards in the pocket of a fat priest of the Roman worship making his way northwards to woo the red dwarfs of the Far North while the ice kept them still, those wanderers. Pere Martel is his name. I have seen him and fed him and sold him goods for silver twice before. He was travelling this time in the cart of a trader who brings me linens from the looms of Ghent. And he'd been given it by a wine-merchant who'd led six wagons with a guard fifteen strong from the Loire to the Wetlands. They were passing through Condate when the merchant was given the letter by an old woman to send it on to me—with haste, she said, before the blizzards set in. But the wine-merchant nearly delayed too long in the Wetlands, offering wine for cloth, finally trading—if the priest's word be trustable—ten barrels of red for fifty ells. A bargain for the wineseller, you may take my word for it. Then the priest moved on and the letter came at last—late, but by good fortune safe, with the cloth-carrier's last cart of the old year. No doubt the letter explains more. I'll get it now and read it to you.'

'Please get it but I'll read it myself.'

'You can read already?' Julius was as disappointed as he was surprised. Now he might never know what news the letter brought, and news was important to him. He was a storer and dispenser of news as much as of goods. Through him, he liked to believe, the world learnt what the world was doing. Besides which, he, like this Viking boy, wanted to *know* what was going on. He tried to hide his disappointment but said testily, 'If I'd been told you could *read* I'd have sent the letter with the daft girl and her father. I wouldn't have bid them fetch you in such a season.'

'I'm not sorry. This mountain of yours is worth seeing.'

'Glad you like it.' Julius clapped his hands again. 'Roxane,' he called, 'bring the letter that came for Mordec son of Hauk.' He did not take his eyes off Mordec. 'You're not in the common run of Viking lads, are you? Not that you look any better than the rest, but at least you wear glasses, and you can read. Or so you say. Let's see you do it. Give the letter to Mordec, Roxane.'

Mordec held out his hand for the square package. Roxane and Julius watched him with eager, curious eyes as he opened it.

the letter

The wrapping was white linen, sewn tight. Mordec used the tip of his dagger to cut the stitches, then pulled out a long strip of goatskin stretched thin. On it the message was written with a sharp quill dipped in oakgall ink, by a hand flowing and easy. He read:

From Lily Queen of the Fenreach to Mordec son of Hauk. Greetings.

I have crossed the sea. I stand on your side of it though far from where you bide among the bees and appletrees near the harbor of the longships.

I crossed before the shortest day on a round and clumsy ship with a Christian priest and hooded men of the brotherhood we call the Black Monks. Often and again for nine months of the year he and they dare the wild crossing between Cornwall and the coast of West Francia.

This I learnt from Isolde who works now in the kitchen of the Earl our neighbour and was sent by him to cook the feast for the King of Cornwall's wedding. A moon-month she was away travelling and toiling among the Brythonic Celts.

Why would the King of Cornwall marry in the depth of winter? A mystery surrounds his haste but

I have no time to find it out. Lady Jessica would have gone to the wedding, taking her ladies and a strong guard, but the Earl her father forbade her to go. Or to speak truly he begged her not to go, saying that the way was long and dangerous, and she heeded him.

It was to Jessica I went when I had spoken to Isolde. I told her I wished to go to Cornwall and cross with the priest and the monks to France and she gave me a full purse which one day I will return to her filled again.

So I set out on Maelstrom my stallion and was on the road for nine days. I lodged at last in the castle where the King had wed, and he was there yet, though he kept out of sight. Odd to tell he was bereft of his bride. None knew what had become of her, or would not say.

The castle stands on a rock at the end of a causeway jutting out towards West Francia, and twice every day the causeway is swamped by the tide and the rock becomes an island in angry seas. When high waves broke beneath my window they flung foam high and on some nights my floor was wetted.

A boatman fetched me away on the day of the sailing. He rowed me in a small boat from the rock to the shelter where the round ship waited.

I had to leave my stallion in the care of the King's men. I warned them not to mount him if they valued their lives. They swore they would not but would treat him well, but I fear he'll gallop off if he can and how will I find him again I wonder.

The round ship rolled on a frisky sea in a rude wind and the priest prayed not to die. I tied myself to the mast and sang though the foam hit my mouth. Now I am in another castle on another rock off the coast of West Francia. The waves break too far beneath my window to wet my floor.

The castle is a tall tower, and the Black Monks are building an abbey against it. In this tower lives a Magician called Sam of the West. He is known far and wide for his power though he is young. Like me he lives with a grandmother. Her name is Djil. She it is who is writing this letter for me. I speak, she writes and then she reads the words aloud. They are not all my own words but they will do. When the letter is written she will send it to you, she has promised me. She knows how it can be borne to your cold dark land and into your hands.

So I will come to the point and then it can start its mysterious journey. My reason for coming you know well. It is to find my mother. To save her from her cruel captors and take her home. Then she and I will raise an army to fight you, you Viking wolves, and keep you away forever from our shores.

So come and fetch me and take me to search for her. I do not know where. You must find out. I asked Sam if he could tell me where to look but he said that though he has great powers he cannot dream where my mother is. So it is you must help me find her as you said you would.

I know you will not break your word. If you do I will find you and cut your heart out. Never forget that your life belongs to me because I saved it. And do not keep me waiting longer than you must.

Come armed and bring others if you can. Gus is one who may come if he will.

a magic bird

Mordec laughed as he read the last few lines of the letter. Whether or not the old woman who wrote it had used many of Lily's own words, these rang true to her nature, which was trusting and threatening, fierce and generous, and brave above all. But what should he do, he wondered.

He looked up at the eyes fixed on him, and said, more to himself than to Julius and Roxane, 'I don't know how to start.'

'What is it you must do?' Julius asked. 'Perhaps I can be of help.'

'Help? I have to find a queen who was taken captive in England and brought to the Northlands.'

'What is her name?'

'Queen Gloria.'

'Who captured her? Come, tell me all, and you will have whatever help I can give you.'

'Well—' Mordec hesitated, looking doubtfully at Julius. 'Yes. Perhaps you could help me. Here—read the letter.'

'Ah,' said Julius, taking the letter and devouring it with his eyes. Then he read it aloud to Roxane. When he'd finished, she spoke to Mordec for the first time. 'Is it true she saved your life?'

'Yes.'

'Then you will do as she asks?'

'Yes.'

Julius said in a puzzled tone, 'You will take a step that could lead to your own defeat in battle and expulsion from England?'

Mordec shook his head. 'It's her dream,' he said. 'It doesn't scare me—us, I mean.'

'Why does she need her mother back to raise an army? What sort of woman is this mother of hers that she could do it better than anyone else?' Roxane demanded to know.

'Queen Gloria? I don't know. All I know is Lily thinks she's what England needs.'

'Judging by the letter,' Julius mused, 'I would say Queen Lily herself has the mettle.'

'She has!' Mordec agreed emphatically. 'But she thinks she's too young to be a leader, and her grandmother, Queen Bertha, too old.'

'There's a high chance that her mother died in the great battle when Eyiolf's forces were defeated and his fortress razed,' Roxane said. 'If so, I pity this young queen. But now the first thing you must do is answer the letter.'

'No sense in that—I'll get to her as soon as a letter would,' Mordec said. 'I'll start when the snow begins to melt. But I don't know how we'll find her mother.'

'Only let her know you have received her letter. That you will come. That you are making a plan. Then make the plan and get ready to go,' Julius advised.

'But who'll take my letter to her?'

'If you are bent on this adventure, Mordec son of Hauk, regardless of what it might lead to, write your answer. There's a messenger here now who will take it.'

Mordec laughed. The Troll was a joker. 'I saw no carts or sledges at your door.'

Julius smiled too and said, turning his head round to face Roxane, 'My dear, fetch the messenger.'

Roxane went out and returned with what might have been a large lantern in a long linen cover. She set it down between Julius and Mordec and pulled off the cover to reveal a pigeon in a cage made of fine gold bars.

'Meet France Southeast, one of my messenger doves,' Julius said. 'He will carry your answer to the wine valley and from there it will be taken to the young queen on the rock.'

Mordec knew nothing of pigeons who would return always to the place they had come from. What made them do it, he wanted to know, and how did they know where to go? Julius answered that the why and how were secrets of magic, and all he knew was that they flew home.

'And when they get there with the letters, who finds them?'

'Men and wives who have my trust. They take the messages where they are meant to go. Now, Roxane will give you paper and ink. Write a short answer and if the wind stays down it will be flown off today, tied with a thread of silk to the leg of my lovely dove.'

'I'm not sure—'

'What to write?' Julius said. 'Ah-hah. I thought that may be a trouble.'

'Alright. I'll say I'm coming to fetch her from the island. And I'll do it. But where will we go from there?'

'Where was Queen Gloria captured?'

'In England.'

'And she was brought across the sea? You're certain of that?'

'Lily told me so.'

'Who captured her?'

'Men who fought for Eyiolf the Bald.'

'Brrrr!' Julius shuddered as most of the folk in the Northlands did when that name was spoken. 'Then your quest will be hard. The tyrant's fortress was laid waste, his watchtowers were burned to the ground, and most of the bloodthirsty beasts in the form of men who fought for him were slain. The remnant scattered far and wide.'

'Is there anybody, do you know, who could say where Eyiolf's son has gone? Lily thought he might have been the one who ordered Queen Gloria's capture.'

'Eyiolf's son?' Julius turned to Roxane.

'Ingolf,' she said, 'was his only son. Or the only one we heard of. Some called him Ingolf Beadthreader, and others, Topspinner. He was nothing like his father, that boy. Soft, very soft. So they said. And he liked to wear feathers, and stir cream into his morning cup of hot oxblood. Ingolf wouldn't carry off an Englishwoman. Couldn't, and wouldn't want to.'

'How d'you know all this?' Mordec asked her.

'I lived in those parts. My father and mother died at the hands of Eyiolf's men. I was hidden or they would have killed me too. Julius found and saved me.'

'There is one man,' Julius said, 'who served the tyrant as armourer and he lives on in these parts. His name I forget. Find it out, seek him, learn from him if you can where Ingolf might have gone. And listen to gossip. I too will ask. And the men and wives I deal with—I'll get them to ask too. Nosing about is the best way to pick up a scent. You'll soon have somewhere to start. Now write. Say you will come to her.'

'Harvald the Armourer?' Mordec said as he followed Roxane to a table where a scrap of paper lay, with quill and ink beside it. 'Is he the man you're thinking of?'

'The very one.'

Mordec wrote:

Mordec to Lily. Your letter in my hands. Will come to you. Awaiting thaw.

Three small men drove Mordec home in Julius's sleigh.

They wore red hoods and cloaks, never spoke at all, and were adepts at cracking very long whips over the team of twelve dogs. The moon was out and the wind rising when the sleigh drew up at the gate of Hauk the Meadmaker.

Estrid, wife of Hauk and mother of Mordec, gave meat and drink to the silent three in the warm house, and fed and watered their dogs, and afterwards invited them to sleep near the fire, but they rolled their heads about to say no, and set off again.

For hours it seemed that the sound of their whips could still be heard, but it was only the wind.

Mordec read Lily's letter to Estrid and Hauk, and told them what he meant to do when the thaw came. He half expected them to be against his going on such an uncertain and hazardous quest, but though Estrid expressed her doubts that it was likely to succeed, and Hauk laughed and said he hoped it would not, neither of them tried to talk him out of it.

From the day of his return home from England last year Mordec had noticed that his mother and father took less notice of him than they used to. They hadn't asked him to repeat as many times as he'd expected the story of his arrest and trial, of how he'd been found guilty on the false charge of plotting to invade an independent territory all on his own, and had been sentenced to death by strangulation and drowning in a bog, and how he had been saved only in the nick of time. Perhaps it was just too painful to them to hear the story told often.

But it was more likely, Mordec complained to himself, that all they thought about these days was his baby brother Eyrin who'd been born while he'd been away in that distant land staring death in the face.

Yet he didn't really resent Eyrin. Sometimes, when nobody else was looking or listening, he told *him* the story.

mordec's men

Ice gripped the land but on the shore there was a hole in the whiteness, a cave. Inside it nine boys huddled round a fire, their shadows cast waveringly on veils of smoke.

Eight of them were listening to Mordec telling them about his letter from Lily, and what he wanted to do when the thaw came. 'If we all go we could sail Foal of the Foam with the first southward-bound trading fleet.'

No one answered. Olaf, son of Olaf the Shipbuilder, had a funny smile on his face, Mordec noticed, as if he knew something he wasn't telling.

Mordec looked at Gus. If Gus said he'd go on this quest, Eric would come too, and the rest wouldn't want to be left out. But still Gus made no answer.

Gunnar said, 'She wants to get her mother home to make war against *us,* right?'

'Right.'

'So why d'you wanna help her?'

'I said I'd help her find her mother, nothing else.'

'But that's the first step to their making war on us.'

'Lily saved my life. You know that. I'm in her debt. So I gave her my word and now I have to keep it. If she makes war on us, I'll fight against her.'

Gus spoke at last. 'You'll have to. We all will.'

Eric, always taking Gus's side, said, 'That's right.' And Titch, Eric's younger brother, said, 'Anyway, it's *your* word of honour, Mordec, not ours.'

Gus said, 'Wait! I haven't said I won't go with Mordec.'

'So you will?' Mordec asked.

'But you can't!' Olaf shouted.

'Why shouldn't he?'

Silence again. Mordec frowned. He was beginning to suspect that something was happening that they didn't want him to know about.

Horsa spoke at last. 'Why don't you tell him? He's gonna know sometime or other.'

'Tell me *what?* Come on. Horsa?' But Horsa kept his mouth shut. 'Gunnar?'

For a moment Gunnar turned his smoke-reddened eyes on Mordec, but looked away again. Gunnar was never one to step out of line.

Mordec looked over the top of his glasses at Eric, but knew he'd get nothing out of him because he'd be sure to follow Gus's lead. And it was also no use trying to get anything out of Titch, because Titch could only do what Eric did, by order of their father. So he turned back to Gus and bawled at him. 'Gus, you stupid ox, can't you open your big ugly mouth and tell me what this is all about?'

'Don't shout at me!' Gus yelled back. 'It just happens that we've got something better to do than go on a wild goose chase because of—some girl.'

'All right then *don't* tell me,' Mordec said irritably, getting up and pulling his cloak over his shoulders.

'I don't want to know actually. Anyway there're plenty of men who'd give their ears to go with me.'

'*I'll* tell you,' Olaf said suddenly, in a tone that was aggressive and triumphant at the same time. 'They're none of them gonna come with you, Mordec, because they're gonna come with me. See?'

'Where to?'

Silence again except for a forced laugh from Olaf.

'Why're you all scared to tell me?'

That goaded Olaf to a hot response. 'Who's scared of you? You may as well know. We're going to sail with Bjarwulf.'

Now it was Mordec's turn to stare. 'Not in Foal of the Foam you're not!' he protested.

'Why not? I knew you'd say that! And that's why I didn't want you to know about it. But she's not yours, you know. Just because you found her you think she's yours. But she belongs to all of us. Isn't that right, Gus?'

But Gus said nothing.

Mordec returned to his place and sat down again. Keeping his voice calm he asked, 'Does Bjarwulf know about this?'

'Our Dad told him,' Titch said.

'And he doesn't mind a toy ship joining his fleet?'

No one answered. The truth was, no one had told Bjarwulf the Pirate that his new recruits meant to sail in their own small craft.

'I see,' Mordec said.

'I'm not going with them,' Big Hengist, the stout boy, said brightly. 'I'd come with you to France,

Mordec. I've heard the food's good and the wine's fit for the gods. But I don't want to go in search of Lily's mother. You could travel about for months or even years and never find her.'

Mordec nodded. Big Hengist wouldn't have been his first choice anyway. He needed strong men about him, willing and able to fight if they must, and Big Hengist was a born cook rather than a born warrior.

Gus would be the best companion on such a quest, and he hadn't doubted for a moment that Gus would agree to come, not just because he and Gus liked each other, but because Gus really liked Lily. They all knew he did, and his coolness when he talked about her didn't fool anyone.

Of the rest it was Horsa that Mordec would have chosen, because Horsa could handle weapons. He was a warrior born and bred, but he'd never said he wanted to go pirating. How had he been won over to Olaf's reckless dream?

Mordec turned to the last of the eight, the one who would have been third on his list because he was clever at inventing and making things: Little Hengist. He was looking at Mordec, expecting the question that came.

'You?' Mordec said testily. 'Are you also planning to throw away your life in a pirate raid?'

Little Hengist shook his head.

'So you think pirating is a waste?' Olaf said, pretending to be shocked by what Mordec had said.

And in a way it was shocking, since a Viking was a pirate by name, nature, calling and reputation.

Pirating remained the sacred occupation, and the one who scorned it was felt to be a kind of traitor to his folk, his forefathers, his own blood.

'Now, yes,' Mordec dared to say, brazening it out. 'It's different for old men of forty.' Then he added teasingly, 'But come to think of it, it wouldn't be a waste of *you* lot. Please go right ahead and have a really good time getting yourselves killed. Now I come to think of it, if Foal of the Foam has to be sacrificed so that you can be fed to the monsters of the deep, it'll be worth it.'

'We're not all going with Bjarwulf,' Little Hengist said. 'Aren't you?'

'No. I want to work with Harvald the Armourer. He can make things no one else can make. He even knows how to make things that move by themselves. I want him to teach me.'

'Why now? You could do that next winter,' Mordec said as he left the cave. He didn't wait for an answer. He wouldn't beg any of them for help. If they didn't want to come with him for the adventure, if they'd rather go pirating or work in a shed, he didn't mind, he'd go alone. And alone it would have to be, since he didn't really know where to find those other men who'd give their ears to come with him.

Mordec sat in the mead hall with Harvald the Armourer, Horsa's grandfather, listening to his tales of the bad old days when he had worked in Eyiolf s fortress.

Mordec asked him what he knew of Eyiolf s son, Ingolf.

It's true, Harvald said, that Ingolf wore feathers, and true that he stirred cream into his morning cup of oxblood. He had once run away with a troupe of dancers from Constantinople. When Eyiolf found out, he was furious.

'Not in the way we'd come to expect, when he roared until we quaked in our boots. This time he'd only just started roaring when he broke down and wept and whined. We'd never seen him weep before. He sent a hundred men to fetch the boy back. I heard that the lad was halfway to the Bosphorus before his father's men caught up with him, cut the dancers' feet off and brought the lad home. I don't think Ingolf felt about his father the way the old tyrant felt about him. How Ingolf escaped the slaughter in the great defeat is a mystery. I think he was helped by the captain of the guard, what was his name—Horick? No, Rorick—that was it. Ingolf had been put in Rorick's charge after the dancing nonsense. Now what was the last I heard of this Captain Rorick? Someone, I forget who, told me he'd gone to Italy, to the old city of Nebulo. Yes, and Rorick might know where Ingolf has got to. But why d'you want him?'

Mordec explained. The old man shook his head. 'Queen Gloria you say her name is? I heard nothing of a Queen Gloria. I'd have thought Ingolf the last fellow in the world to seize a woman, any woman. Also, you see, he wasn't a very brave lad, even if he did risk his father's fury now and then, and I'd expect only an unusually brave and reckless man to carry off a queen.'

'Perhaps this Captain Rorick did it for him?'

'Ye-es, it's much more likely that Rorick would snatch her,' old Harvald said, 'but I don't believe he'd have done it on orders from Ingolf.'

'On whose then?' Mordec asked.

Harvald looked at him for some moments, a smile in his eyes. 'Perhaps on the orders of the queen herself,' he said at last, and broke into a loud cackling, the nearest thing to a hearty guffaw the old man could manage, while he banged his drinking-horn on the table to signal that he wanted it filled again.

'Now he's saying silly things because he's drunk,' Mordec thought, so he said good-night and went to bed.

setting out

With a mixture of surprise and relief, and a pinch of hurt, Mordec came to see that neither his mother nor his father would try to hold him back from the long, uncertain and dangerous journey he told them he must take.

'Be sure you travel with others who know how to keep themselves safe,' was their only instruction, several times repeated, but always while their eyes were fixed on the cradle where Eyrin lay.

'If you go to Italy and you're anywhere near the town of Brevis, you'll visit your grandfather there, won't you?' Estrid said.

When icicles started dripping heavily in the first rays of a pale sun, Mordec began to prepare for his journey, sewing gold coins—his share of Eiyolf's treasure found last year in England with Lily's help—into the hem of his tunic.

He told Gus, Horsa and Little Hengist which day he'd be leaving if the weather remained good. None of them had anything to say about it. But when the set day was near, Little Hengist came to Mordec's house and announced that he'd decided to come with him.

'Good,' Mordec said. 'Don't bring more than you can carry.'

And then, when the day itself had just dawned, and they'd loaded the cart and the old dappled mare stood ready in harness, Horsa strode up calling a cheerful 'Good morning!'

Like Mordec and Little Hengist he wore a sword as well as a dagger. Saying nothing about why he'd changed his mind, he dropped his bag, a second sword, a bow and a sheaf of arrows into the cart.

Mordec asked no questions and made no comment, but when they'd settled themselves among their things gave him a friendly clap on the back.

Hauk, showing no surprise at the sudden appearance of a third traveller, took up the reins and clicked his tongue. The mare started off and Estrid stood at the gate and waved good-bye.

'If you see Father tell him how fine a boy Eyrin is,' she called. Mordec raised an arm in farewell.

Thin films of ice still lay over the mud-puddles in ruts of the rough road and they cracked under the onslaught of hooves and wheels. Spring it might be, but it was still cold enough to make the travellers wrap their furs closely about them.

It was with a train of fur-buyers who still expected at that time of year to make sales of their merchandise both in the Wetlands and the north of France, that they were to set out from The Troll's mountain.

Julius and Roxane greeted Mordec as an old friend, which he almost was by now, having visited them twice to find out about traders' arrivals and departures between the time he had fetched Lily's letter and this morning when he was starting out to do what she'd asked of him.

The Troll and his lady regaled them with wine, meat and fruit. The meat tasted good, and Mordec could not tell, did not ask, and was not told, whether it was aurochs, ptarmigan, or dog.

Hauk had brought gifts of apples and honey, as well as ten casks of mead by way of payment—nine for the carriers, one for Julius. He asked Julius how he came to have grapes at that time of year, but Julius either didn't hear or deliberately changed the subject. Hauk did not need an answer to conceive the idea that he might bring some of his produce here to the mountain, to be stored and sold to visiting traders or exchanged for their goods.

Hauk stayed to watch the boys depart in the last of the fur-carrier's ten carts, drawn at a slow but steady pace by a pair of young ponies. He count-ed the guards: twenty of them, and he wondered whether there shouldn't be more, and whether they carried weapons enough. They wore French chain-mail under long cloaks of scarlet wool which they spread behind them over the broad haunches of their heavy mounts, and seemed to be strong and steady men, but there could be no certainty of it.

Reminding himself that there was little he could do to ensure the safety of his son now or ever, Hauk stopped worrying and drove home with his head full of the new idea Julius's trade had put into it.

the bad and the frightful

The travellers kept on the move for only a few hours, then stopped for the night.

In a corner of a cold barn faintly lit by rushlight, the boys sat on cushions made of their own furs wrapped round straw, took food from their bags and set it out on the damp floor. Mordec had many small meat pies which Estrid had cooked and packed for him, and stacks of flat bread, apples in coats of hard red honey, and white cheese. He shared his good things with his two companions, whose hard bread, hard cheese and smoked spiky fish punished their mouths.

Darkness grew, almost as thickly inside the barn as out. Men and boys rolled themselves in furs and slept.

Outside, the guards kept watch five at a time. Mordec listened to them stamping, coughing, and spitting the night mist out of their throats. For a long time he lay thinking about the quest he was rashly undertaking, the perilous ways they'd have to travel. He was beginning to doze when he was startled awake by a shout. A moment later it was repeated. He couldn't understand the language of the guards but he was sure that what he heard was neither a challenge nor a command, but simply a name flung into the darkness: 'Borrel'. From the distance another name, 'Molay', came flying back. Quietness followed, and then again the stamping, coughing and spitting.

Next day Mordec told the driver of the cart what he thought he had heard.

The driver was a thin, tall, gloomy, staring man who shaved his jaws every few days so his lower face was almost always black. He dressed all in black, and added to his height with a tall narrow hat made of bark. His name was Thorp.

'You heard right,' he said, and went on to say that the guards and the brigands were all the same sort. 'If the brigands could get work as guards they'd be glad to have it, and if our guards didn't have this work they'd be brigands. But them being a band of brothers, they don't attack each other, see, and that's what keeps us safe for now.' At any moment, he believed, they could all get together and 'that would be the end of us'. No guards, he warned, were ever to be trusted. But then, who in the world, he asked, was to be trusted? 'It's a sad, bad world,' he said, 'where I can't trust you, and you won't trust me.'

Twice that day, as the train wound through forest, the guards chased off would-be attackers, turning their great horses awkwardly among the trees as they gave chase, aiming their spears but unable to hurl them any distance without striking boles or branches. The enemies were not men but packs of lean slavering wolves with scarlet snarls who appeared on all sides at once.

The boys joined the chase, though the guards laughed at Mordec and Horsa's home-made bows and arrows and Little Hengist's catapult. But on the second chase it was Little Hengist alone who killed one of the beasts. His stone hit it between the eyes and it yelped once, leapt up and fell. Mordec and Horsa cheered and the guards lost their laughter and stared at the boy in astonishment. They asked to see the weapon that could shoot with such speed and force, and Little Hengist let them inspect it. It was his own invention, he explained, showing them how he had inserted springs between the iron fork and the strings of gut and oxhide.

They stopped that night at a village and found shelter in houses. Sent by a cautious housewife to the far end of her dark room, far from the hearth, the boys opened their bags to take out the evening's ration of food and Mordec found his bag empty. They had no choice but to make do with hard bread and hard cheese.

As he lay down to sleep the sudden thought came to Mordec that it was Thorp who had pilfered his food when he and the others had left the cart to chase the wolves.

A chance arose next morning for him to search the man's baggage. Not long after they'd set off across wide, flat country, Thorp put the reins in Little Hengist's hands, jumped down from the cart and went off on some errand of his own. As soon as he was out of sight Mordec pulled out Thorp's bundles from under the driver's bench, searched them, found what he was looking for, and put everything back in its right place, his own boxes and parcels in his own bag. He decided to say nothing to the man about the theft.

When they stopped for the night he found most of his food still there in its wrappings. Though the leaves were dry and wrinkled and the pies and bread harder, it all tasted good enough to the three ravenous boys. When they'd eaten their fill, Mordec peered round the barn for mournful Thorp. He saw the lanky figure sitting against a wall with his eyes shut, the bark hat beside him on the floor.

'Thorp,' Mordec called, 'catch!' The hooded eyes sprang up, the skinny arms stretched out and the fingers caught the piece of pie which was flung at him like a scrap to a dog. He examined it closely for a few moments, licked it tentatively, and then gobbled it, looking across at Mordec as he chewed, but not uttering a word.

The boys exchanged glances, Mordec winked, and silently they lay down in their furs. They felt pleased with themselves. Men such as they were not easily bettered, was the drift of their thoughts. They also felt full and contented, and soon slept soundly. It occurred to none of them to keep watch on a man who was now their enemy.

And in the night Thorp crept over and put a barn rat into Mordec's bag, in the hope that it would devour every last crumb.

The train set off again in a red dawn. At first nobody spoke, but when the sun broke out so did the guards' chatter.

A little later, warmed and cheered, they struck up a song. The boys didn't know the language but they liked the tune and began to hum it, and then, led by Mordec, they made up their own words to go with it.

'A thief should be captured and tied up in bonds,' Mordec sang.

Thorp's long narrow back remained stiff.

'Hung on a willow and strangled with fronds,' Horsa went on.

'Tied to a stake and stifled with leaves,' Little Hengist added.

'Vikings will show him what happens to thieves,' Mordec ended.

Soon it was too hot for singing. There was only the creak of the wheels and the stamp of hooves.

A guard at the rear called out something that made the other guards laugh, and one turned round to reply but stopped as soon as he'd begun, the smile dying on his face. He cried out and pointed and the rest turned to look behind them.

What they saw threw them into panic and confusion. In a frenzy of whipping, the horses were turned off the road and driven, carts rocking wildly, into the sparse shelter of trees and bushes. Driven through thorns, the boys raised their arms to protect their faces, and felt their sleeves catch and tear. From all along the line came groans and yelps, but the guards made shushing sounds, and issued hoarse, harsh orders which silenced them. Men went to hold the ponies' heads and stroke their noses to keep them from snorting. The boys jumped down from the cart with a thump which brought out another hiss of shushing from the guards. Then all waited tensely behind the flimsy shield of branches, the guards standing one-foot-forward with arrows in their bows and the bowstrings taut but not yet stretched.

The boys hadn't had time to scan the distance for a glimpse of whatever it was the guards had seen, but they heard a drumbeat, regular and hard, and a shrill whistling, and harsh bird-like cries.

Far from frightening them, these sounds made their eyes light up. They stayed where they were though, crouched and peering to see what was coming towards them. When they saw clearly what it was, they looked at one another and smiled.

Yet it was a hideous train. A small cart came first drawn by a bullock which was led by a tall yellow-haired youth. In the cart a pole had been raised and supported by props and cords, and a ghastly figure was impaled on it. Slit open from throat to belly, its ribcage was opened wide into two rectangles of white and red stripes like the wings of a bird of prey, revealing the innards, all jammy black bags and bloody tubes. One of the pink, flayed legs ended in a shoe, but the other seemed to have lost not only the shoe but the foot, and from the stump a chain hung down swinging as the cart swayed. A ragged cloak was tied round the neck and hung behind the otherwise naked trunk of the cadaver. Under a crumpled cap, the face protruded as if it had been made of hot wax and pulled into a funnel with two gaping holes. But it was not the distorted face of a man. It was the ordinary face of a pig.

A long wagon followed, drawn by four plodding oxen with their noses close to the dirt and driven by a giant on a high bench. He wore a cloak of thick wolf's fur fastened at his neck with a silver moon. His helmet had a leather nose-piece. His thick moustache and the braid hanging from his chin were bright yellow.

Scuffing along behind the long wagon came a tinkling line of healthy, well-fed, yet dissatisfied slaves, roped to each other from waist to waist, men, women, boys and girls, their wrists and ankles chained.

And behind them walked free men who all, except the drummer, beat every bush and tree trunk within reach with the flat of their swords, and at the same time kept up the racket, whistling and shrieking like sea-birds.

They were the guard, yet they wore no armour, not even helmets, and carried no shields. This was a signal to all who saw them that they feared nothing and needed no protection, because of what they were, what they were capable of doing and habitually did in unquenchable bloodlust. Their reputation was their shield, and the corpse on the pole was a reminder of it. Beware, it said.

And it wasn't the only warning sign. Along the sides of the wagon hung rotting chunks of flesh, guts, offal—a panoply of blood.

The boys had seen enough now to feel perfectly at ease. Mordec grabbed the shoulders of Horsa and Little Hengist on either side of him to lever himself to his feet. He charged past the guards, through the hedge and on to the road, and to the shock and fury of the crouching fur-carriers, stood in the path of the advancing train waving his arms above his head.

He didn't know how close he came to his end at that moment. Perceiving him as a cowardly traitor, a guard raised his bow, stretched the string and aimed, and only Mordec's shouted 'Hullo!' and the calm and cheerful look on his face stopped the release of the arrow. Could the lad see more through his glasses, the guard wondered, looking again at the advancing train, than the rest of them could see with their naked eyes?

The giant on the hideous wagon called back, 'Who are you?'

'Mordec son of Hauk, travelling south with fur-carriers.'

No sooner had he said his name than the tall yellow haired youth abandoned his place at the bullock's head and came running towards him.

'It's Gus,' Horsa said to Little Hengist. They struggled out through the branches to stand beside Mordec.

'So you changed your mind,' Mordec called. 'Or did Bjarwulf send you home?'

Gus stopped and said, breathing hard, 'I knew I'd catch you up. If wolves or cutthroats didn't get to you first.'

Mordec said, 'Tell us—did you grab much loot? What happened to the others? Lying at the bottom of the sea, I s'pose? Foal of the Foam sunk and lost, I s'pose?'

'Wrong. We didn't go. Bjarwulf's not sailing until the summer. And I know you need me to lead you.'

'You mightn't get back in time to sail with Bjarwulf.'

'That won't matter. I can live a heroic life on the land as well as the sea.'

'So that's it—you're here to live a heroic life. And I thought you might just have decided to help us find Lily's mother.'

'That's exactly what I've come to do.'

'You'll help us look for the lost queen?'

Gus nodded.

'Thought you might,' Mordec said. 'Lily will be pleased.'

But Gus had nothing to say about that. He turned his eyes away from Mordec's.

By this time the giant had driven near enough to pull up the oxen and halt the whole train. One of the Viking guards leant back against the bullock's nose and pushed until the beast stopped.

'Who're these boys?' the giant asked Gus.

'They're the ones I came looking for.'

By now several of the Frankish guards had emerged cautiously and were standing with their bows pointing down, though they kept the arrows on the strings.

Horsa turned to them. 'It's all right,' he said. 'These are Vikings.'

The guards didn't seem much relieved by this news. Mordec said 'Truly, they won't attack. They're traders, not raiders.'

The fur-carriers emerged then, leading the ponies and carts, all except Thorp who was nowhere to be seen.

The boys went to look for him and found him hiding in a hollow log. He didn't move when they called to him so they reached in and pulled him out. He trembled and was almost unable to speak. Staring at Gus he managed to stammer 'P-please d-don't—'

'Don't what? What's he think I'm going to do to him?' Gus asked the others.

'Oh nothing much,' Horsa said lightly. 'Just the *usual*. Bind him, hang him, strangle him—'

'Tie him to a stake, slit him open, splay his ribs—,' Little Hengist said, shrugging.

'Why would I want to do that?' Gus asked, looking the stick of a man up and down and seeing no reason to help or harm him.

Thorp stammered, 'It wasn't m-m-me put the rat in the bag. I saw it go in, I didn't stop it, but it wasn't m-me. P-please don't—'

Mordec had no idea what he was talking about.

'We might not kill you,' Mordec said, 'if you're very good to us forever more. And you will be, won't you, old man?'

'Yes,' Thorp tried to say while swallowing hard, the lump in his throat bobbing up and down.

'Well, go to the cart then. Get ready. You'll have four of us in it now.'

Thorp loped off to do as he was told. The first thing he did was open Mordec's bag to let the rat escape.

By the time the boys returned to the road, the leader of the fur-carriers, Lothair, had arranged with the Viking giant, Svavar, to keep their trains together as long as they were travelling in the same direction.

This plan proved good for Lothair and his men. For the rest of the journey, no robbers or cutthroats came near them. There was no shouting of names at night. The smell of the rotting offal was horrid, but it warned off beasts of prey. At the same time it attracted carrion crows. A growing flock of the black birds flapped overhead day after day.

Now Mordec had to buy food in the villages for himself and his men. At first there was nothing to be bought but black bread so hard it needed soaking for an hour if it wasn't to break their teeth. And it didn't take their hunger away.

The slaves were better fed than they, on thick messes of pulses, twice daily to keep their value up. Gus asked one of their guards to give him some of the porridge, but the man warned him off with a bird-shriek and a raised sword.

On the fourth day they reached a small market town, and that night the boys feasted on chickens and eggs, ale and new cheese. Leftovers stored in their bags stayed there. Jugs of fresh water appeared beside them night and morning.

the torrents of spring

Each day as the sun shone longer and hotter it melted more ice in far invisible hills, and streams poured down to the plains.

The travellers could hear all about them in the grasslands and the forests the noise of rushing waters, swelling to the tumult of rivers in spate. Big rivers overflowed and bridges were swept away in the floods of spring.

Three times the double train had to turn east or west and lose a day in search of a safe crossing, sometimes through swamps where wheels sank into mud and could only be pulled out when the men and boys added their strength to the power of the oxen and the horses. The drivers grumbled. The boys were reminded of the English fens, though these swamps were wider and shallower.

The Viking guards told fireside tales of hideous creatures lurking in the swamps, man-eating monsters with claws, scales, poisonous fangs, and an everlasting hatred of mankind.

They came at last to green valleys. The carrion crows vanished from the sky. And when the first vineyards fanned out on either side of the road, exciting the wonder of the boys who'd never seen them before, the two trains parted company.

The Vikings put away their ghastly warnings, their guards donned armour, and Svavar took his human merchandise on to the far south.

The fur-carriers with their passengers turned west. Smoothly on wide and easy roads they moved, passing below the white walls of castles topped with graceful towers on which pennants of many colors fluttered in the warm breeze.

Mordec and his men climbed down from their cart for the last time in the market-place of a large town and took up their loads of bags and weapons.

'Be good now,' Mordec said to Thorp, by way of farewell.

'We'll know if you're not,' Little Hengist called cheerily.

'Remember, we Vikings are everywhere,' Gus said darkly.

Thorp stared ahead, upright and steadfast in a treacherous world.

the red magician

In response to their shouts, a sailboat came across the short stretch of sea to fetch them; a beautiful little boat painted white, its sails rose-colored, its seats marble, its boatman a plump boy with brown curly hair and round blue eyes. Smiling, he held the boat to the landing stage while they jumped on board.

'My name is Arnulf,' he said. 'I come from Allemagna. I used to be a robber but soon I'll be a soldier because I've joined the Army of the Redeemed and I'm going to war.'

'Who's your enemy?' Horsa asked. 'Who's invaded your land?'

The boatman held the handle of the rudder under his arm as the breeze swept them towards the island under a cloud-soft sky.

'Nobody's invaded. I'm going to fight the heathens,' Arnulf said.

'Who're they?'

'Folk who're not Christians.'

'*We're* not Christians,' said Gus, gripping the hilt of his dagger.

'Oh I know who *you* are. I've been told. But you're not the sort of heathens we're going to fight. Yet.'

'Why're you going to fight them? For loot?' Horsa asked.

'I hope so,' said the ex-robber, 'but mostly we're going to fight them just because they're not Christians. The Black Monks go to all the castles for miles about and get brigands like me out of the dungeons to send against them, and we don't mind because we'll cut their throats and chop their limbs and stick swords in them and take what we want and no one will do anything to us. The Pope and the Emperor will even pay us to do it.'

'Maybe the heathens will do something to you,' Little Hengist said.

'Like what?'

'Cut your throat and chop your limbs and stick swords into you.'

'Oh they can *try* but they won't beat *us*,' Arnulf said confidently, 'because we'll have God on our side.'

Horsa, Mordec and Little Hengist looked at each other and laughed. And Arnulf joined in pleasantly.

'Tell us about the magician,' Mordec said.

'Sam of the West? What d'you want to know about him?'

'First of all who calls him that and why?'

'Everyone calls him that. There was a magician in these parts who had the gift of second sight and could see where everything and everyone was on earth and in heaven, in the past and the future, and he was called Zarath of the East. Then when Sam was still a boy, folk said he had the gift too, so they called him Sam of the West.'

'What happened to Zarath of the East?'

Arnulf didn't know.

As they neared the island they saw some of the Black Monks standing on ledges of the rock at various heights, their faces invisible inside their hoods. Mordec felt their silent watching was unfriendly, even menacing. They melted away as the boys stepped ashore.

From the foot of the rocky mountain Mordec gazed upward, shading his eyes against the cloud-glare. He saw the abbey, some of its walls still only half-built, and workmen climbing up and down ladders. On one side, rising sheer to above the highest peak, was a white tower.

'The only way up,' Arnulf said, pointing to the start of a path, and with a nod and another sunny smile he left them. They began to run up the slope, then steep steps, but soon they were trudging, and by the time they reached the door of the tower they were panting for breath.

Mordec expected the tower to be cold inside, bleak and wind-haunted, like the one in England where he'd been imprisoned. But he found it quite different: warm and carpeted.

A servant clad in yellow led the boys up its wide stairs to a large round bright room where Lily was waiting for them. She was dressed as they best remembered her, in boy's clothes.

She ran to Mordec, flung her arms about his neck and bit him quite hard on the ear in her happiness at seeing him again and to show how glad she was that he'd kept his promise.

But at the same time she was looking over his shoulder to see who else had come, and it was to Gus that she spoke first.

'So you're here too,' she said, and looked away, as if it hardly mattered one way or the other. 'I thought you *might* come but I wasn't sure.' Gus's face reddened as he answered with no more than a grunt.

She turned abruptly to Horsa and said, putting her hands on his shoulders, 'You're welcome, Horsa son of Harvald, because you're a sword-master, and we'll have to fight. And Little Hengist, it's good that you've come too.'

Little Hengist met her dark eyes, which always looked out intensely, even fiercely, from under the straight eyebrows.

'Please just call me Hengist,' he said. 'Big Hengist isn't here so there won't be any muddle. And that goes for all of you.'

He glared round at the other boys and Horsa grinned and said, 'Alright Little—I mean, Hengist,' and he pushed his fist hard but playfully into his friend's shoulder, almost unbalancing him.

They followed Lily to the top of the tower where Sam the Magician was at work. To the boys' surprise he was only a few years older than themselves. His features were fine, his skin fair, his hair the colour of dark red amber. He was dressed all in red. On his feet he wore red silk slippers.

He was happy to see them. 'You've survived your travels unhurt, as we kept hoping you would.'

'We had a Viking escort most of the way,' Mordec said. 'The look of them terrified brigands and wolves.'

Sam took them down to another room where his grandmother, the Countess Djil Gaudin, sat on a bench and worked making a tapestry. She was dressed in black with a white veil over her grey hair. She looked up and smiled as she greeted them courteously.

She listened to their names, her eyes moving from one to the other. So Mordec was the big one who had hair of many blond colours, wore glasses, dressed in dark blue, and was, she knew from Lily, literate and clever.

Of the others Lily had said nothing and Djil sized them up as best she could on a first meeting.

Gus the tallest one, yellow-haired, bold-eyed, strong and serious, was probably a natural leader of men.

Horsa the sturdy one, with hair the colour of hay, had a watchful but candid look in his light brown eyes which suggested that he was brave but not impetuous.

The character of Hengist, who was thin and wiry and had limp pale hair and green eyes, was harder to guess, but she supposed that he too might be clever.

Lily went to sit on the bench beside Djil, and men-servants in yellow tabards appeared suddenly as if conjured out of the air to place chairs for the visitors.

Three lean grey dogs slunk to the space before the hearth and lay down in a row, chins on crossed paws.

Mordec began to tell Lily what he'd heard about Captain Rorick and no sooner was his name out than Lily leapt up with excitement and cried out, 'That's the one! Rorick was the name of the captain that Eyiolf the Bald sent with his son to take my mother away. Where is he, this Rorick?'

'Last heard of in Nebulo and Ingolf may be with him. And if we find them we may find out where your mother is.'

'May? Must! Well come on then. We know where to go so let's go.'

'Not now, not today, my dear Lily!' Djil said. 'They've come a long way. Let them rest awhile with us.'

'We'll try to prepare you as best we can for your journey, and that will take a little time, a few days at least,' Sam said.

Mordec looked thoughtfully at the powerful magician. 'Lily wrote that you can't tell us where Queen Gloria is.'

'That's true. I have no power of "second sight". By reputation I have, but I haven't. They say I'm a magician, but nothing I do is magic. I play with things and watch what happens, that's all. Some of the effects seem like magic and stories about what I'm doing are spread about and everyone who hears them adds a little bit, so by the time the stories come to the ears of the monks who share this rocky island with us, they've often become very fantastical. Now and then the Abbot comes to see if I'm practicing witchcraft. But I get him to play with things too, and he enjoys himself, though he won't admit it.'

Over the next few days Mordec was to discover that although Sam was modest about his powers, he already knew more than most people could reasonably hope to learn in a lifetime. And to know things, Mordec understood, is to have a kind of power.

He and Hengist chose to spend most of their stay on the island with Sam in his workroom, a watch-tower of the sea and sky.

'I observe the weather,' he explained to Mordec and Hengist, 'the formations of cloud, the tides, and I keep records. Fishermen ask for my predictions before they put to sea. I tell them what the skies portend, and when tides will be high and low, and I always explain *why* I say that this or that will happen, yet they go on believing that I have "second sight". I warn them to watch out for sudden events of nature that cannot be predicted, but to them that only means there are other magicians in the sky or the deep who are even more powerful than I am.'

He showed them some of the things he played with and watched. From his roof-beams hung seven globes of iron in a row, seven of wood, and seven of glass; the iron on ropes, the wood on thongs, the glass on silk threads. In each row Sam could make one globe move at the end of the line without touching it, by lifting the one at the other end and letting it go to strike the next in line. Then it was as if a message was sent through one after another to the last one, a command, 'Swing out!'—and swing out it did. Whether the globes were glass, wood or iron made no difference to the trick. 'Now you do it,' Sam said, and Mordec found that he could work the wonder just as well.

'Why does it work like that?' Hengist asked, also making it happen. He picked up two of the iron globes and let them hit the third—and two swung out at the other end.

Sam replied, 'I don't know. All I know is that it works every time, as if by a law that can never be broken.'

He had many books. Mordec pored over volumes on History, Law, Nature, Philosophy, Mathematics. He asked Sam which of them told the truth, and which did not.

'Because some books don't,' he said. 'I was given one, a Bestiary, by an English priest, and I don't think it contains a word of truth. But I like the names of the beasts and their pictures make me laugh, they're so different from all the animals I've ever seen. Can you tell me, Sam, if these beasts exist?' And he wrote a list from memory.

Sam read it and said, 'You're right. They're mythical, most of them. All of them probably.'

'How d'you know?'

'No beast can have both feathers and fur, nothing can eat stone, no lizard can have hair, no hairy beast can have a bird's beak or webbed feet, no bird can have a shell, no snake can have wings, no cat can have hooves. I can't explain why not, but some day we'll know why things are as they are. With living things I guess they need to be like this or that because of *where* they live and *how* they live. If they were different they couldn't live as they do, so they wouldn't be there. Something like that.'

MORDEC'S LIST OF BEASTS

Mordec didn't know the meanings of the Greek and Latin names, but Sam did. They're given here in English.

- *hopligats* — hoof-cats
- *venenoprobats* — poisonous sheep
- *glarries, var.:* — seagulls, various:
    - *glarry citroonyx* — the yellowclawed gull (also called the *unguitogryph*)
    - *glarry prasinonyx* — the greenclawed gull
    - *glarry erythronyx* — the redclawed gull
- *anapterogyps* — wingless vultures
- *trixadraks* — hairy dragons
- *iffypodscyls* — web-footed dogs
- *petraphageleons* — stone-eating lions
- *chrisospinosaurs* — gold-quill lizards
- *trixadraci* — hairy serpents
- *rubesims, pol.* [popularly known as]
    - *ruberogs* — red monkeys
- *sclerochins* — hard geese
- *maurocerodorks* — blackhorn deer
- *bodermasus* — ox-hide swine
- *ramphiarctos* — beaked bear
- *rhinoceros* — [beast with a] nose horn

Mordec thought this made sense. Sam always made sense. He never pretended to know what he didn't, or to be sure when he wasn't, but he plainly knew a lot. Mordec asked him if he could be his prentice one day, when the quest for Lily's mother was over.

'I'd be glad to teach you,' Sam said, 'but I'd ask you to find other masters too. There are learned men in Italy who know a lot more than I do.'

Later he told Djil that Mordec was not yet ready for a long course of learning, that he was restless and drawn to action, but one day, when he was tired of voyages of discovery, he'd be a fine prentice.

'He is a Viking after all,' Djil said. 'And yet—it's not often I meet a man or boy who likes knowledge and ideas as well as adventure. He told me he can read and he likes books. He's probably not of pure Viking descent. My guess is that he also has some other blood in his veins.'

Neither of them asked Mordec about his ancestors, but one day Mordec told Sam, 'My mother's father is not a Viking. He lives in Italy.'

'What is he then? And where in Italy does he live?'

'He's a Lombard and he lives in a town called Brevis in Lombardia.'

'I see. The trouble with Brevis is that it's not fixed in one place.'

Mordec tried to imagine a town floating in the air, but told himself at once that Sam couldn't be meaning anything so unlikely.

'And Lombardia,' Sam went on, 'is always only an abstraction.'

'What does that mean?'

Sam explained: 'There was once a race called the Lombards, or the Long Beards. And they had a kingdom. But they were defeated in war with the Emperor Charlemagne and their kingdom ceased to exist. Now the word Lombard does not mean a race of men. It means an occupation, a profession, and Lombardia is and will be anywhere, everywhere. It is anywhere that Lombards work, and being one of them is a matter of what you *do* rather than what you are by birth.'

'I still don't understand.'

'You see, they are men who are wealthy and powerful but without owning land or herds, or armies or fleets. They can, and they do, move whenever they feel threatened, and what they take with them are documents, records, books with names and numbers in them, the numbers being sums of money.'

'Are they magicians?'

'You could say that, if minds working well are magical.'

'Are they bad men?'

'What do you mean by "bad"?'

'Do they break their word?'

'No. They need to be trusted, so they don't break their word. In other ways, some are good and some are bad, like men everywhere. What they *do* is good. If more men used their services there'd be less bloodshed on the roads. Travellers could go anywhere with just a piece of paper in their tunics instead of sacks of coins. The piece of paper would be written by a Lombard in the town you came from, let's call it Mordectown. It would have your name on it and his, and it would instruct another Lombard in the town you go to, let's call it—'

'Hengisttown,' said Hengist who'd come nearer to listen.

'—to give you, and only you, the money you need. It's called a letter of credit. Then when *another* traveller went the *other* way, he'd carry a piece of paper from the Lombard in Hengisttown. So eventually everything owed would be paid back. Of course the travellers would have to pay real money to the Lombards in their own towns. But they wouldn't need to carry it on roads beset by robbers.'

'And if a robber stole the bit of paper?' Hengist asked.

'It would be no use to him. To turn it into real money he'd have to pretend he was the man he stole it from. And that wouldn't be easy. He'd need to read and write, which not many robbers can. And then he'd have to answer questions about the man who'd signed the paper, and he wouldn't be able to.'

Mordec thought about all this and then said: 'If I bought things in Hengisttown and took them home to Mordectown, the robbers could steal the *things* from me while I was travelling.'

'True,' Sam agreed. 'There would still be danger on the road. But not as much as before.'

'So that's what the Lombards do. They sign these papers.'

'Yes. But that's not all they do. They also help traders to borrow money, and the lords of great estates, and farmers, and kings, and even the Emperor and the Pope.

Of course, no single one of them is rich enough to lend all the money, so they do it as a group. The group is what people mean when they speak of Lombardia.'

'And this group is living now in a real town called Brevis?'

'The Lombards live in many towns and cities. But most of them are living now in Brevis, where it stands for the present.'

'Is it far from Nebulo?'

'Let me show you on a map,' Sam said. 'We'll chart a route from here to Nebulo that goes by way of Brevis.'

But this was not the work of a moment. Sam said he would send to the towns on the mainland for travellers' tidings, news from Italy, reports of the roads, and word of ships due to sail east from the southern ports. Mordec and Hengist were happy to wait with Sam for as long as they might.

The map of the known world that Sam showed them in his high room held their gaze for many hours. They'd never seen one like it. Sam said it had taken him years to draw, and he still wasn't sure how true it was. But he thought it was right enough as a broad picture of the lands of the Franks, and of Andalus, Italy, Sicily and the Empire of the Byzantines. Hengist wanted to know how distances on the ground were made small on the parchment and Sam began to explain, writing down numbers.

But Hengist confessed that he couldn't read. So Djil taught him. He learnt fast, and wished he could stay longer to learn more.

Sam too wished that Hengist could stay. He could see that this boy's skill at devising and building things was greater than his own. One evening Hengist said to him, 'I've been watching the seagulls. They row with their wings to fly, but they can also hold them out and just lie quite still in the air. I think I know how an airship could be made that would fly like that, gliding on the aircurrents.'

'Come back one day and we'll build it together,' Sam said.

In the evenings food and wine were served to them of a kind which 'the gods and Big Hengist should taste,' Horsa said.

Mordec conceded that the cooking was even better than his mother's who was 'the best cook in the Northlands'. And never, he said, 'not even in England with noblemen and knights', had he drunk such wine.

While they dined Sam talked about the future, how it would bring flying ships and other marvelous devices.

After dinner they played boardgames new to the boys. And Djil told them words of the language spoken in that part of the old Frankish kingdom. She had been brought up at the Emperor's court 'and there I learnt many tongues,' she said.

She questioned Lily and the boys about their lives. Mordec told her how he had found the small ship and what had happened to him in England. She listened attentively, and asked about their homes, their houses, parents, neighbours, the things they used and how they made them, their food, and the stories told by the skalds.

She said she would weave pictures of their lives and stories into her tapestry.

lily and gus

While Mordec and Hengist spent their days with Sam, Lily and Gus rode and raced strong horses on the mainland, within the domain of the Gaudins. Hengist remarked to Mordec that the two of them 'seemed to get on better than they used to'. Mordec only laughed.

Each morning soon after sunrise the two of them were taken by Arnulf, the robber boatman, across the water in the white boat with the rosy sails, and each evening fetched them back to the island.

Once as their horses walked on a beach, Lily said, 'Three years—that's how long I think it will take for my mother to get a great army ready to defeat you.'

'Will your mother really be able to unite the rulers of England?'

'My mother is the one person who can do it.'

'And you believe that her army could force us out of England?'

'Yes. That's what we'll do. I've told you. Do you dread the battle?'

'Of course not. I want to fight and win.'

'But I know that *we'll* win.'

'If I thought there was a chance that you'd win I wouldn't help rescue your mother. Even knowing that you could never defeat us hasn't stopped me thinking sometimes that helping you is treacherous.'

'Does Mordec feel the same?'

'It's different for Mordec. You saved his life.'

'So will you turn back and let Mordec and the others go on with me? Or do Hengist and Horsa also feel like traitors?'

'I don't know. I haven't asked them. But no—I won't turn back.'

'Good,' said Lily.

'There's something else I've been thinking,' Gus said. 'That there's another way you can become the free ruler of your land.'

'What way? There's none but war and victory.'

'Or war and defeat.'

'How can defeat make us free?'

'You go to war against us, we win—which I know we will—and then I marry you and we rule the Fenreach together.'

Lily laughed, and watched his face redden. Then she said, 'If ever I want to be married, Gus, it's you I'll ask. But only if we win.'

Not wanting to hear another word from him on the subject, she kicked her heels into her horse until he galloped, and left Gus far behind.

Next day as they paused on a high hill Gus said, 'If your army makes war against us, I'll seek you out on the battlefield and we'll have to fight each other in single combat.'

'Why? Do you want me to kill you? Because that's what I'd have to do.'

'Or I'd kill you,' he said.

'Yes. Or you'd kill me. I'd never yield. So it must be a fight to the death—yours or mine.'

'Yours. I want you to know that you're the last person in the world I want killed, yet I myself will have to kill you. It will be a story of heroes. The skalds will tell it until the world dies.'

Again she laughed at him. Sometimes, like Mordec, she found things funny that Gus felt were grave or even sacred matters.

In the taverns of the market-town where the horses were stabled, they'd quench their thirst at evening with warm green wine which the vintners' wives tapped from new barrels. And they'd listen to the talk around them, much of it about the Army of the Redeemed.

Villagers and peasants, urged by the Black Monks to join, told each other why they couldn't possibly do it.

None said it was because they feared the Black Monks, but if ever they spoke of them or the Abbot, it was in hushed tones and with fear in their eyes.

This the riders reported to their friends in the tower on the island.

the black abbot

'Why do they fear the Abbot?' Mordec asked.

The boys were alone in their sleeping-chamber, yet Gus whispered as he replied, 'For his cruelty. The folk round here say he has a torture chamber and even tortures little children.'

'Why are you whispering?' Horsa asked.

'Sh! They say he has spies everywhere.'

'You think they can hear through walls and doors?'

'Why not?' Mordec said.

Two days later Horsa was approached by the Abbot. Horsa had found his way to the monks' armoury and made a friend of the chief armourer, who was not a monk but one of ten professional soldiers they employed.

One morning Horsa, while hefting a well-made spear with a fine appreciation of its quality, joked with his new friend that if he were a Christian he would go with the brigand army that the Abbot was forming to fight the heathens, because he'd never yet used weapons in battle. The armourer laughed and told his fellow officers what 'the young heathen Viking had said'. Someone carried Horsa's words to the ears of the Abbot, Brother Alonso de Llama. That august personage did not laugh.

He came to look for Horsa in the armoury, sliding in with soundless tread and standing so still that when the boy saw him at last out of the corner of his eye he started, wondering how long the monk had been watching him. From the size of the jewel-studded crucifix which this particular monk wore on his chest, Horsa guessed it was the Abbot himself. What he'd heard about him was enough to make him wary of the man.

But Horsa was cool and restrained by nature, seldom impulsive, not easily shaken, so his voice and manner were calm as he said 'Good-day'.

The Abbot's silence continued for some moments, until Horsa had almost given up expecting words to issue from the funnel of the black hood. When they did, they came in a cold tone.

'Good day, my son.' As he spoke the Abbot pushed back his hood to reveal a delicate narrow face as pretty as a girl's, crowned with golden curls half-circling a bald pink pate. His cheeks were smooth, his lips cherry-red, his eyes an almost violet blue.

'Can someone who looks so—so sweet,' Horsa asked himself, 'be as cruel as they say he is?' And at once, in his thoughts, he could hear Mordec answering 'Why not?'

The Abbot asked Horsa to walk with him in a courtyard among the half-built walls, and as they strolled up and down Alonso de Llama talked about love.

He said that everything he did was for the sake of love, and sometimes the things he had to do were terrible. War was terrible, but—'Love requires it,' the Abbot said solemnly in his cold voice, turning his violet eyes to Horsa who looked away, said nothing, and put a hand on the hilt of his dagger.

'I hear,' the Abbot went on, 'that you are eager to do battle?'

'When I have to,' Horsa said.

The Abbot said no more about it for the present. He spoke of other things for a turn or two, then let the boy return to the armoury.

But again the next day Alonso invited him to walk in the courtyard. As they picked their way through the rubble and round the ladders, the Abbot talked about love and Horsa held his dagger.

On their third crossing, the Abbot urged the boy to submit himself to baptism and so become a Christian, stressing how valuable a soldier he'd be 'for the Cross'.

'Give me time to think about it,' Horsa said.

'You *will* think about it?' the Abbot asked, trying to catch Horsa's eye and failing. Horsa nodded, but kept looking away from the Abbot.

Back in Sam's tower, Horsa reported what the Abbot had asked of him. Sam said the Church, with many people like the Abbot in it, wanted total power over everyone's lives. 'In another few hundred years,' years,' he said, 'it will have reached into every land and every home and enforced its will with iron and fire.'

At last the route to Nebulo through the port of Genova and by way of Brevis was charted. 'But be ready,' Sam warned, 'to change any part of the plan at any moment if you find things are not what you expect.'

'I shall miss them,' Djil said to Sam as the time of their departure came close, 'especially Lily and Mordec.'

'They will come back,' Sam said to comfort her, and because he too hoped they would.

to castle sec-et-doux

Feeling the sadness of separation, Mordec looked back at the receding island and the dwindling figure of Sam standing on the shore with one arm raised and the three grey hounds beside him.

Djil was crossing with them to the mainland. For the next three days she would tour her domain to inspect her lands, villages and fortifications. For this she was sturdily clad with a leather apron cross-strapped to her chest and looped up from the ground, and wooden pattens on her feet to keep them out of farmyard mud.

But first she would take Lily and the boys to the castle of her neighbours on the south-eastern side, the first direction of their route.

Lily, wearing two Viking swords captured by her grandmother, sat with Djil on the marble seat in the bows of the boat, and a silent Arnulf held the rudder. A small fleet of similar boats, all with rosy sails, came behind them over a calm sea under a clear sky, bearing attendants.

What Horsa saw as they drew away was the hooded figure of the Abbot standing motionless on a ledge of the rock.

'He means us harm,' Horsa said to Gus.

'Who? The Abbot?'

Horsa nodded.

'Two of his monks climbed into the last boat,' Gus told him.

On the mainland a group of domain servants awaited them, and a wagon with a pair of geldings between its shafts. Lily and the boys climbed into it to ride with Djil. Her reeve trotted beside them on a polished roan, and servants, some of them armed, came after them on donkeys.

Dogging the procession were the two Black Monks mounted on mules.

Horsa asked Djil, 'Are they coming to keep watch on us?'

Djil said, 'Certainly. On you, on me, on all of us. The Abbot believes that everyone is plotting to slip out from under the eye of the Church in order to smash down the pillars of the world in wild and sinful glee. But he has no power over me and Sam, or over our serfs or peasants, or the freemen of the towns in our province. Not yet. Maybe one day the Church will extend its power over everyone in the world, as Sam says it will try to do. The Abbot would like that. At present, fortunately, the Abbot himself has power only over his portion of the rock. We didn't want to sell any of it to the Order, but we had little choice. We sold it under pressure from both the Pope and the Emperor. Each of them has his own reasons for wanting to please Alonso. The Pope would use his army and the Emperor fears it. And they were both happy to be rid of his nagging envoys. Now we live in the shadow of Alonso's dark wing. We could leave the tower and move to one of our other castles. But Sam wants to stay where he is for the sake of the work he is doing.'

'The Abbot wants power to do terrible things in the name of love,' Horsa said. 'It's hard to understand. Eyiolf the Bald wanted power to do terrible things, but not in the name of love.'

'We also cannot understand it. Who can? It is madness. Once the island and the tower were our refuge from men who torture and kill just because they can. Such men mean to do bad, they like doing bad. But another sort have arisen, who torture and kill to do good. They will make our bodies suffer to save our souls, they say. The Abbot is one of these. So now Sam and I must protect ourselves from the onslaught of the good.'

Mordec laughed sympathetically, shaking his head to show that he too thought the Abbot's mission beyond understanding.

Lily, who usually liked his laughter, gave him an angry look.

'You laugh, Mordec son of Hauk! You should be making a vow to come to the aid of Lady Djil and Sam of the West. What is the use of being born a warrior if you cannot do battle where battle is needed?'

She took Djil's hands in hers and said, 'When my mother and I have driven *them* out of our land,' and she nodded at Mordec, 'we'll come and fight for you.'

'Thank you, dear, if I need you I shall let you know,' Djil said.

'The only protection a ruler ever has is the strength of her arm, her armour, and her army,' Lily declared. 'And if you have no army, then you need allies.'

It took them half a day to cross the Gaudins' lands and another three hours to reach their neighbours' beautiful castle.

When they got there Horsa noticed that the two monks who had followed them most of the day had disappeared.

In a splendid hall Djil presented the boys to the lord and his wife, the Duc and Duchesse de Sec-et-Doux, who had wine and wheaten cakes served to them and invited them to stay there that night, promising also to set them on the road in the morning with an escort as far as their own southern border.

When Djil was ready to set off again she embraced them all and put a small bronze casket in Lily's hands.

'It holds charms for you and the boys,' she said, as her reeve helped her back into the wagon. 'I cannot say that they are truly magical,' she added, smiling wryly, 'but they do have a certain power. They could save your lives. Just hang them round your necks when you need to.'

When will that be?' Lily asked.

'You will know, my dear,' Djil replied, and waved as she was driven away.

When they opened the casket they found silver crosses on silver chains.

the doll

The Duc de Sec-et-Doux was a gloomy man who had become sad early in life through contemplating the fate of butterflies. 'To live in all their beauty for but a few months!' he would lament to anyone who'd listen to him.

His wife was a severely practical and impatient lady, somewhat older than he, who because of the Duc's melancholia carried the whole burden of government and administration on her own shoulders. She even sat behind her husband in his court of law to tell him what judgments to pass. She had borne him two sons and sent them off, as soon as they were old enough to bow with grace, to serve the Pope, so that they would not come under the 'watery influence' of their father.

Under her management the estates were prospering, the fields were fair, the wine flowed. Everywhere, the Duchesse told her visitors, *fortification et village* were in good repair, and the coffers of the Duc were full and many.

Once a month the Duc and Duchesse banqueted their officers and neighbours, the high churchmen of the region, and interesting travellers.

The Duchesse liked to hear accounts of life in foreign parts, was taking an active role in recruiting villains and vagabonds for the Army of the Redeemed, and frequently announced that if she were a man she would lead an army of conquest across the sea to conquer the Holy Land from the infidels, and no one doubted that she would.

The night Lily and the boys spent at the Castle was a banqueting night and a large crowd was expected. Everyone except the Duc, who withdrew to be sad in peace and quiet, bustled about preparing for the evening's entertainment.

The Duchesse busied herself with preparing Lily for it. She had never had a daughter, the now ageing Duchesse de Sec-et-Doux, and wishing that she had, she seized whatever opportunities came her way to mother sweet girls of any age up to thirty. If a sweet girl was lacking, a strong and sturdy one would do, so she made the best she could of Lily. She brought her a gown like the starry sky on a deep blue night, and jewels for her throat and arms and hair.

Lily duly admired the gown and jewels, and let servants bathe her in scented water and dress her hair and deck her in the finery. Not for a moment did she let the Duchesse see that she 'felt like a colt pretending to be a cloud'—as she was to tell Mordec and Gus next day when they were far from the beautiful castle. One of the boys was to tell her some years later that he'd liked, and would never forget, the way she'd looked that night.

The entertainers amazed everyone, but none so much as Lily and the boys.

A strong man, announced by a herald as Igor the Rus, lifted a horse with three acrobats on its back. Next, to the music of drums, flutes, and a stringed instrument, a tumbler walked and danced on his hands. Jugglers followed, and then came a troupe of dancers like lords and ladies except that the lower parts of their legs were bare. They were crowned with model sailing ships, nests of birds, flower gardens, sleighs, piles of fruit, castles. They came in whirling on their toes and stopped all at the same moment in a circle. Into the middle of it a rag doll about the height of a ten-year-old child was tossed. It lay limply with bent limbs.

Igor the Rus came and picked it up, swung it, flung it high, caught it, dropped it. It slumped on the floor. Igor and the dancers bowed and went out. The music stopped.

Then a drum began to beat again. With each beat the doll twitched and stiffened and straightened a little until it was sitting up. Suddenly, on a drumroll, it flew through the air as if it had been plucked up by an invisible hand and chucked away in anger. It landed in a heap.

The strong man came and picked it up by an arm, slung it over his shoulder and walked off with it.

Everybody clapped. The ladies called out that they wanted to know how it was done.

A priest, whose face was flushed with fury or fear or wine, demanded that the Duc find out if they had been forced to watch the workings of witchcraft.

In came the strongman again with the doll over his shoulder, swung it down, and it stood on its own two legs. With both hands it lifted off its 'head' of rags to reveal the smiling face of a girl.

She bowed. Her hair, dark as soot, fell in a tumble of curls round her shoulders. Her laughing eyes were as black as eyes could be and mischievously bright.

The priest sat down as if his legs had been knocked from under him.

The boys looked at each other and when Mordec started to laugh the others did too.

Applause came loud and long as the girl skipped away.

in sombre wood

Bright and early Lily and the Vikings set out on the next stage of their journey accompanied by the Duc's head groom, a stern person, and also some stable lads and an English maidservant who'd been sent as a present to the Duchesse by a sorceress of London. All the servants were liveried in tabards 'the colours and patterns of butterfly wings', as the maid pointed out to Lily.

But Lily hardly heard her, so taken up was she with curbing the urge of her borrowed mare to turn about and go home again. The wayward animal soon gave in to her rider's stronger will and fell into line behind the groom, who led the party. He and the Vikings were mounted on pale fear-eyed steeds recently broken in, while the butterfly servants sat low on shaggy ponies.

For some three hours the procession wound among vineyards to reach the south-eastern corner of the domain.

'That way,' the groom snapped—a man who grudged words except to horses and his master the Duc, whom he deeply respected for his melancholy. The wide straight dusty road he pointed to with his willow-crop curved away round the base of a hill.

The boys dismounted, hung their bags on their shoulders and started along it in a straggling line while the stable lads took up the reins of the pale steeds to lead them back to the stables.

'My lady,' the maidservant whispered to Lily as she helped her with her bag, 'has anybody told you of the Warning Beasts in Sombre Wood?'

'What're they? What about them?'

The girl intoned rather than said, '*Don't go into the Sombre Wood,* for *if* you go into Sombre Wood and you see the Warning Beasts, *you should go not a step further.*'

'Why not?'

'Why? Well—because.'

'Because what?'

'Because it's a sign, my lady.'

'Of what?'

'Of *danger.* The sight of them means, *don't go on.* Turn back, or else.'

'Or else what?'

'Disaster, my lady.'

'And they appear only in Sombre Wood, these Warning Beasts?'

'Yes, my lady.'

'Then I *must* go into the wood, mustn't I? I must go and look for them, so as to be warned—if there's danger ahead for me. D'you see?'

'Yes. I s'pose that's right, my lady.'

Just then the priest who'd feared that witchcraft worked the 'rag doll', rode up on a snorting, sneezing nag of his own. He patted the maidservant on the head as he trotted past her, and when he was beside Mordec slowed his horse to a walk.

Smiling he asked, 'Did they tell you about the short cut? No? Then let me set you on it. Follow me.'

He veered off to the right, and Mordec, seeing no reason to refuse, followed him.

'No no!' Horsa shouted from the back of the line as the others stepped off the road and headed through long grass towards a dark wood. Near the first trees the priest reined in his windy mount and pointed to a path.

'Quick way to the valley,' he called, nodding and smiling. 'Once there you'll not lose your way.'

'But wild beasts—,' Mordec said. 'Wolves?'

'None here. Perfectly safe,' the priest said, then turned his mount, waved cheerily and trotted off.

Mordec was well in among the trees when Horsa caught up with him.

'Not this way,' Horsa said. 'We must never do anything churchmen tell us to do. Let's go back to the road.'

But Mordec went on, Lily and the others followed, and Horsa did too, giving up trying to turn them back.

The path was soon lost in fern and bracken, gorse and nettles, and the light was dusky. A thin sound of pipes, scarcely different from the sigh of a breeze, sounded eerily in the depths of the wood. They stopped to listen and were startled by a bird's shriek, followed by the growl of a beast.

They stood looking about them and through the screens of leaves appeared heads and bodies, claws and horns and tails, wings and beaks. Dreadful creatures were snuffling and rustling in the thicket. They were surrounded by monsters.

'The Warning Beasts,' Lily said. 'This is an enchanted wood.'

She and Horsa drew their swords, Gus his dagger, and Hengist folded his arms and looked about him with a frown. Mordec burst out laughing. 'Don't worry,' he said, 'they're not real. There are no such beasts as these.'

'What are they then?' Lily demanded.

'People,' Mordec said. The branches dropped back into place, leaves swished together and the beasts were gone from sight.

'How d'you know?'

'Cock's head with eagle's wings and lion's legs?' Mordec said. 'Goat's horns on a big purple lizard? Bat's wings on a begging dog?'

'Could be,' Gus said.

'Couldn't,' Mordec contradicted him bluntly, shaking his head. He felt all the more sure of himself on this question since his talk with Sam. 'In any case,' he added, 'different kinds of beasts don't herd together.'

'How do you—'

'Sh!'

Gus fell silent and Mordec dashed into a clump of bushes and came out pulling a bright red woollen monkey.

'Look what I've caught—a ruberog!' Mordec called. He took the creature by one arm and its tail and swung it from side to side. It yelped and chattered its teeth until Mordec set it down.

'Let's see you,' he said. The monkey's red woolly hands came up and lifted its head off to reveal a human head with dark hair and a girl's smiling face. It was last night's little dancer, the living doll. She put a woolly monkey-thumb to her nose, wiggled her monkey-fingers at them, giggled, ran to a tree, leapt up, and reaching out with one arm grasped a young beech-branch which promptly broke. She fell on her monkey-tail in a crackle of breaking gorse. 'Ouch!' she yelped.

Mordec helped her up.

'I'm too hot in this,' she said, smiling again as soon as she was safe on her two feet, and she began to pull off the ruberog-costume. But she had nothing on under it, so Lily dressed her in spare garments of her own which she cut down to size with her dagger.

When the girl was clothed in the jagged buckskins, she sat on a fallen tree with her captors to share their bread and wine.

Her name, she told them, was Charlotte. She'd been with the troupe of dancers for as along as she could remember and though none of them were her kin they'd treated her well. But now she was tired of that life and would stay with Lily.

'Forever,' she said, 'or a bit of forever.'

She couldn't answer Horsa's question about who it was had told them to dress up like beasts and ambush them in the woods.

'I don't know *who*,' she said, 'but *someone* paid Timble—that's our leader—to make us do it so you'd be too frightened to go on.'

'Someone who doesn't know Vikings,' Gus said.

'This Timble,' Lily said. 'Won't he come after us to get you back? Will he expect us to pay for you? You aren't worth much to us and you certainly wouldn't be worth the bother of a fight, and in any case we've got to get on. We don't have time to waste over you.'

'I'm not a slave,' Charlotte said. 'He doesn't own me. Nobody owns me. You're not going to own me either.'

Lily looked at her for the first time with a touch of real interest. 'That's good,' she said.

'It must have been the priest who paid him,' Horsa said, 'on orders from the Abbot. That's why he sent us this way. I said we shouldn't listen to him.'

'But why'd he do it?' Mordec asked.

'He wants me in his clutches,' Horsa said, baring his teeth like an angry dog. 'He thought if we were scared enough we'd turn back.'

'Whoever it was, they can't know much about Vikings,' Gus said.

'Or about me,' Lily said.

'Listen, I *said* I'm *staying* with you!' Charlotte shouted, pinching Lily's arm.

'No! You're no *use* to us,' Lily snapped, elbowing her aside. 'You're too small to look after yourself and *we* don't want to bother with you. We've got enough to do.'

'I may be small, but I'm nearly fourteen. And you *must* take me with you. You *need* me because you're a queen,' Charlotte wheedled. 'I know you're a queen because the sad Duc told me. He told me you are looking for your mother who is also a queen. And I know that queens need ladies to attend them.'

'You're not a lady,' Lily said.

'But I'm tired of being a dancer and I want to come with you.'

'Too bad,' Lily said. 'You should stay with the other dancers and move from court to court. You'll be given gold and silver. Your fame will spread to every corner of the world.'

Charlotte thought about this for a few seconds.

'Well, maybe one day I'll go back to them,' she said. 'When I'm tired of you. Please let me come with you to find your mama? I'll do anything you like—paint your clothes, scratch your back, sharpen your teeth, drag your bag, smooth your hair.' To prove her skills she began to press Lily's hair to her scalp with hard strokes of her little hands.

'Get off,' Lily said. 'If you really want to serve me you can go and find out from this Timble who it was who paid him to try and frighten us and put us off our quest.'

'He'd never tell me. And besides, while I'm gone you'll start without me.'

'You're not obedient enough to be my serving lady. There's my bag—try carrying it.'

Charlotte heaved the bag on to her back and bent double under its weight.

'See?' Lily said. 'You're too small.'

'Give it to me,' Gus said, taking it from Charlotte. He tangled its straps with those of his own and hung them both on his back, seeming not to feel the added weight. 'Now let's move.'

'And me?' Charlotte asked, insistently.

'Just keep up with us,' Lily said. 'If you don't, no one will turn back to look for you. If we're attacked you must watch out for yourself. And from now on you must always do what I tell you.'

Charlotte smiled happily.

'And stay behind me, not too close and not too far.'

'I will,' Charlotte said.

'And stop chattering,' the queen commanded.

on a moorish ship

The travellers' way south lay through a long, deep, river valley.

Heeding the warnings of fellow-travellers in the markets where they bought bread and wine and fowls and sausages, they were careful not to walk in plain sight along the riverside road, for the lords of the stone castles on the cliffs above the ravine kept watch for travellers and would sweep down and demand a toll with threats of maiming and slaughter.

So the Vikings, the young queen and the little dancer took winding ways among boulders, reeds and saplings.

One night to keep himself awake Hengist etched a picture of his imagined flying machine on a cave wall where someone else had etched wide-horned humpy cattle, and this drawing was to prove a puzzle and annoyance to ologists in later centuries.

On the last lap of the journey they moved more quickly because of an idea of Mordec's. They'd seen groups of lepers walking openly along the roads, their faces and limbs bandaged with dirty blood-soaked rags, their sticks and crutches hung with tinkling bells to warn of their coming. As nobody dared to touch them for fear of their terrible disease, they passed unmolested on their way.

Except, that is, for one group, whose bells were stolen while they napped in the shade of willows on the river bank. That unkind deed was done by Mordec. He crept among the sleepers, picked up each bell by its clapper, sank it softly in a wooden pail of water, and bore off his loot to a hiding place on the mountainside where his companions waited.

They were tearing garments to make rags. 'What shall we do for blood?' Charlotte asked.

'We've plenty of blood in our veins,' Lily said, applying the point of her dagger to her own shins. 'But you can have some of mine,' she offered gruffly.

And so it was as lepers, wrapped filthily and horribly from head to toe, they safely reached the southern shore. They dropped their bags on a beach and ran laughing into the sea, where the waves and currents unwound their bandages and the tide floated them away. Then they ran on the sand until they were scorched by the sun.

They were granted passage on a nine-sailed Moorish ship, larger than any vessel they'd ever seen before. It was returning from Andelus where it had delivered silks and spices, to Tyre, with no cargo until it reached Genova, so paying passengers were welcome.

Mordec paid a gold piece for each of them except Charlotte, because when she told the captain that she was a dancer he said she could pay her way by dancing when the stars came out.

He was a handsome man, the captain, though he had no visible ears, just a hole on each side of his head. Dark of skin but grey-eyed, he was sumptuously dressed in wide silk breeches striped red and blue, a white silk shirt, red leather boots, and a white headdress with a white plume pinned by a ruby brooch. He wore jewelled rings on all his fingers and both his thumbs. One of his front teeth was coated with gold.

He also wore a short curved sword, sharp on one side only, a type the northerners had not seen before. It was called a scimitar he said. Horsa offered to exchange one of his own swords for it, but the captain refused, saying he'd not part with it, for it was 'better than any Frankish sword'.

He spoke many languages which he'd learnt, he said, 'in a hundred ports, from a thousand lovely ladies'. He told his passengers he was a prince of Baghdad, that he loved the sea, and owned eight vessels like this one.

For much of the voyage, as day after day the stately ship rode the calm swell of a kind sea, he sat in the stern on a leather-seated chair of carved and gilded oak, issuing his orders. Fifty swarthy sailors carried them out under the nine-tailed lash of a stocky bosun who sang like a woman when he wasn't whipping the crew.

'Let me hold the scimitar,' Horsa begged one evening.

The captain smiled, his gold tooth glinting in the late low sun. 'Wait, my friend,' he said, 'and I'll let you do more than that.'

He gave an order to a huge fellow, naked to the waist, whose skin was as deep a brown as dark ale, and whose regular station was behind the captain's chair. The man strode off.

'A Nubian. And he has no tongue,' the captain told the boys.'

'Why not?' Mordec asked.

'Because I had it cut out,' the captain said, shrugging lightly.

The tongueless giant soon returned with a big bald yellow-skinned blue-eyed man swathed in heavy chains. Pushed to his knees at the captain's feet, the yellow man sat back on his heels and stretched his chained wrists towards the captain, babbling words which could only mean a plea to be set free. The captain ignored him.

'This man is a pirate,' he told his passengers, pointing down at the pleading man with a look of scorn and distaste. 'He and his shipmates tried to board us on our last voyage. They would have killed every one of us without mercy and seized our ship and everything in it, but we beat them off. I myself killed five of them with my beloved scimitar, but I spared this man and took him prisoner to learn from him as much as I could. He's told me all I want to know—where their havens are on these shores, and up the Bosphorus and down the Gulf of Hormuz. And soon I and my brothers will equip a fleet of war, a thousand ships and fifty thousand men, and we'll hunt the pirates everywhere, burn their ships, seize their ill-gotten treasure, stain the wide waters with their blood and cleanse the civilized world of this evil. Now the time has come for this man to die, and you, Horsa son of Harvald, may have the pleasure of killing him. With this.'

He laid the scimitar reverently on the deck. Horsa picked it up. He held it high in his right hand and with his left touched the jewels in it, but his face showed no excitement or delight. Then he looked at his fellow Vikings. Their faces were as stony as his own. The same thought was in all their minds: 'What—kill a man in cold blood because he was a *pirate?*'

Even Mordec who had no wish to take up piracy could not help but hold the calling in high esteem.

It would be different if the man could defend himself. Of them all only Gus was an impetuous fighter, but he would balk at becoming a mere executioner.

Horsa in particular was restrained by nature and training from the reckless use of arms. He knew that to fight well, to waste no power, the good warrior does not let himself be easily provoked, and does not lust to kill. Though he must strike when he means to with all his strength, terrible swiftness, and to deadly effect, he must never lose control of his balance or aim or motion, and never abandon judgment if he were to keep the honour of his arms—unless of course he was one of those rare Vikings who went berserk and could slay whole battalions in mad fury without being scathed, because they were chosen and protected by a god.

Horsa turned back to the captain, who smiled and nodded encouragingly. 'Go on,' the captain said. 'Cut off his head. See how sharp and neat is my beloved.'

'Captain,' Horsa said, 'I ask a boon. You know I come of a warrior race. I want to test this weapon of yours and I'd like to kill this man with it—but in combat. Will you unchain him and let him fight me?'

The captain stopped smiling and looked puzzled. 'You'd rather risk your life against his than just slice off his evil head?'

Horsa nodded and the captain gave one of his light shrugs. 'Very well,' he said. He ordered the Nubian to raise the yellow man to his feet and unchain him.

The prisoner watched his chains being unlocked and unwound with a look of fear and wonder, and when they were put aside and he felt the lightness of his unbound body, he stared round the ship and at the sea, seeking a place of refuge, a chance for life and freedom, however slight. But he caught Horsa's eye fixed dangerously upon him and, deciding that valour was the better part of discretion, stayed where he was.

'With what shall we arm the darling?' the captain asked.

'A sword,' Horsa said, putting his hand on his own but at once determining not to lend it to a barbarous stranger, nor risk being wounded or killed with his own weapon.

'No,' the captain said thoughtfully, 'he is not worthy of a sword.'

'But he must be armed,' Horsa insisted.

'I know what to lend him,' the captain said, his smile glinting again, and again he turned to the Nubian with an instruction.

The ebony giant padded away and fetched the stocky bosun who without saying a word handed his nine-tailed whip to the captain. The captain flung it down in front of the prisoner.

'Begin!' he ordered, settling himself to watch by leaning an elbow on the arm of his chair and his head on his hand in a thoughtful pose.

The Nubian went to his usual post behind his master's chair, the passengers stepped back a few paces, and the bosun ducked behind a cluster of bales and casks.

The yellow man took up the whip. Horsa slashed the scimitar about in the air, finding the stroke that best suited its shape. With his feet planted firmly apart and his eye on the curved blade he seemed to be concerned with nothing but the rapid mastery of the weapon. But a question still troubled him: did a whip count as a weapon? Then he thought, 'No more of that—the man will use it as lethally as he can.'

'Let the gods decide,' he shouted aloud, and again he swung the scimitar, this time to cut and kill.

The fight was soon over. As the yellow man whirled the tails above his head the curved blade sliced through his wrist. Hand and whip dropped to the deck. He gaped with horror at his stump, and the blade came down again and cut off his head.

Lily, Gus and the captain cheered first, then Mordec and Hengist. The bosun sprang out of his shelter yelling for sailors to come and clean up the mess. The body, head, and hand were dropped overboard.

Warbling high and sweetly the bosun washed his lash in a barrel of brine which he then emptied over the deck. A sailor set to work on the boards with a mop, and the bosun set to work on the sailor with his whip.

Horsa laid the scimitar at the captain's feet. Its blade was perfectly clean. So sharp it was and so swiftly had it done its work that not a drop of blood clung to it. The captain squeezed the young warrior's shoulder and smiled at him with admiration. Slowly Horsa's grim look changed and he smiled too, with pride.

Then the captain looked up at the sky.

'The stars are out. Dance!' he ordered Charlotte, and she did.

Moments later drum and pipes were playing for her, and the captain clapped his hands in rhythmic pleasure. As the music quickened, so did the feet of the little dancer.

'Wine!' the captain called, and before long he was dancing too, and Lily and the Vikings were stamping, prancing and laughing—none as wildly as Horsa who was usually the calmest and steadiest.

At some point which they were not to remember they fell asleep on the deck, the girls in a coil of rope, the boys on the bare boards.

The captain was carried to his bed by the speechless Nubian, and the musicians went back to their mariner's chores, under a weary lash.

a viking bars the way

They landed at the port of Genova on a mild and pleasant morning, and set off for a walk of some hours along the route charted for them by Sam which would take them through hilly country to Brevis.

The road stretching north-east from the town was wide, as straight as could be reasonably expected through the foothills of a mountain range, its miles marked off by stones on the verges. The Romans had built such roads in England, Lily told Charlotte—who was keeping up well on her short but slender, nimble legs—and Charlotte let her finish before she remarked that she'd been told all about Roman roads by Timble.

'Why did he do that?' Lily asked.

'He taught me lots of things besides dancing,' Charlotte said, 'even numbers and letters.'

'So you can read?' Lily asked enviously.

'Not words,' Charlotte said.

Sam had expected this road to be busy, but they passed three milestones without seeing another traveller. Then, coming over a rise, they saw an armed warrior standing in the middle of the way ahead. Though he stood straight and firm they could tell from a distance that he was old, and drawing nearer they saw a lined face and grizzled beard.

The edge of his breastplate was chipped by rust. On his head was the leather helmet, much battered, of a Viking.

He had the height of a Viking too, being taller than Mordec and Gus and much heavier. Age could not have shrunk him much if at all. He did not move as they approached. His feet were planted firmly apart. His right hand rested on the hilt of his sword as though to bar their way by force if necessary. But he returned their greeting in a friendly tone, and asked, 'Who are you and where are you bound?'

Gus stepped forward and replied in a proper and respectful manner, 'I'm Gus son of Hakon. With these friends I'm bound for Nebulo.'

'I am Lily, Queen of the Fenreach.'

'Lily? And I took you for a boy! But what is an English queen doing so far from home! And this sweet child—your little sister?'

'No. My name's Charlotte and I'm the Queen's attendant. I used to be a dancer in the courts of the nobles of France, and I danced for my passage on a Moorish ship.'

'So young, and so distinguished! And who are you?'
'Mordec son of Hauk. Will you tell us your name?'
'Brinjolf son of Aevar.'
'A wanderer?'
'An exile, but no longer a wanderer. And who is this?'
'Hengist son of Hengist the Fisherman.'
'And this?'

'Horsa son of Harvald the Armourer.'

'Harvald the Armourer? Odds-bods! He must be almost as old as I am. And you're his son?'

'No—you must be thinking of my grandfather Harvald who was armourer to Eyiolf the Bald.'

'Right! The very man! Still at work is he, arming new waves of warriors?'

'He makes no arms for men,' Horsa replied with truth and discretion. He knew that Eyiolf had threatened his armourer with dire punishment if he made armour for warriors other than his own, and that even though Eyiolf was long gone, old Harvald would not defy him, fearing that the tyrant's arm could strike from the haunts of the dead. And because of his grandfather's fears, he would not tell an old Viking warrior who might have been a member of Eyiolf s army that the fine and effective weapons they carried *had* been made for them by old Harvald, though as mere 'toys for boys'.

The old man turned and walked with them along the ancient road in the growing warmth of the day. He said they must have guessed by his remembrance of Harvald the Armourer that he himself had been in the service of Eyiolf the Bald, and he still bore a sword made in Harvald's smithy.

Asked by Mordec whether he knew a captain of Eyiolf's army named Rorick he replied 'Rorick—Rorick—O yes, I do remember', but added that he had long since lost sight of him. He knew there were a few thousand survivors of the routed army, 'but how many of them are still alive,' he went on—his voice unusually strong for an old man—'or where they have found refuge and peace in their dotage, I know not. Except for a very few. One hundred and thirty-one to be exact. Yes, I and a hundred and thirty others live on in a refuge not far from here. Will you come and rest with us for a time before you continue your journey? We'd be glad to hear news of our homeland.' He laid a friendly hand on Gus's shoulder.

Gus exchanged a glance with Mordec. They didn't need to remind each other that it would be a breach of custom to refuse the hospitality of the old man, and anyway they could do with a rest and a meal. Mordec nodded. Gus looked at Lily who also nodded, so he replied, 'Yes, thanks, but we can't stay long.'

'This way then,' Brinjolf said, leading them off the road.

'You're in a hurry, are you, to get to Nebulo?' he asked. 'On an urgent mission, are you?'

'Yes. We're seeking Lily's mother, Queen Gloria.'

'Ah, a quest. But how did Lily lose her mother?'

'She was captured in England by Captain Rorick and carried off to Eyiolfs fortress, perhaps on the orders of his son Ingolf.'

'On the orders of Ingolf? Ingolf son of Eyiolf? That seems, if I may say so, most unlikely. Ingolf was *not* a man of violence. Definitely not. *Not* a man of action. *Not*, as I remember him, much of a *man* of any sort. If Rorick carried off a lady it would be for himself, not Ingolf.'

'We've heard that Rorick is still in his service,' Lily said. 'So if we find Ingolf we may find Rorick, and Rorick may tell us where my mother is.'

'And you know that Ingolf is in Nebulo?'

'We heard he is, and Rorick too.'

'Well, well, you don't say! Fancy that! And I never caught even a whiff of a rumor about their being in Italy. Just as well, just as well. We veterans of the long wars have no wish to meet the son of our old master. Eyiolf was a very hard master to serve, as you must know.'

The old man sighed.

'Nor,' he went on, 'do we crave a reunion with any of Eyiolf s chief officers who may be still in the land of the living. They were hard men too. Youth could endure that hardness, even thrive on it, but not old age. And we need no reminders of the past. Enough that a sadness is always with us because we can never return to our homeland, being as we are, Viking warriors who did not perish in battle with our comrades. Tell me, do *you* despise me now that you know who I am?'

'Yes,' said Gus, still behaving correctly.

'Yes,' said Horsa.

But Mordec took a line of his own. 'If you weren't killed you weren't killed,' he said.

'What are you talking about? If he wasn't killed when so many were and almost the whole army was destroyed, he should have killed himself,' Gus said righteously.

'Quite right, my son, quite right,' Brinjolf said, warmly approving, as he guided them towards a grassy hill.

the theatre of the final days

Brinjolf was spry as well as sturdy, and he led them briskly up a slope between two ancient brick walls stretching the height of the hill. Under their feet they could feel ridges, old steps now covered with grass. At regular intervals on either side, stood large round stones on ledges in a straight line down the slope. Once, Brinjolf told them, these ledges had held statues of the gods, but they'd long ago been carted off to adorn private villas, and someone had replaced them with the stones.

At the top they found themselves on the rim of a large hollow lined almost all the way round with tiers of stone seats.

'See,' Brinjolf said. 'Here's where we live. This is the theatre of our final days.'

In a raised part of the floor there was an opening and as they watched, an old man, not in armour, emerged from it into the sunlight. He went to sit with some ten or twelve other old men in the shade. Two of them were playing a boardgame.

Brinjolf went on, 'It's a grand and spacious hall and very lofty.' He pointed to the open sky and laughed. Although he had not spoken loudly, the old men must have heard him because they looked up and laughed too.

'You live underground?' Mordec asked.

'We store things underground, and sometimes we sleep down there for shelter or safety, but we live and eat and talk and play hnefatafl in this grand space which the Romans built. In those times actors came here to act out scenes from history and legend. Folk would watch and laugh and cry. But no longer. Folk round here don't use it for anything any more, or care what anyone does with it. Come on down.'

'How do you live? What on?' Lily asked, as they descended tier by tier.

'We have sheep and fields, and slaves to tend them, and mulberry groves, and chickens. Filthy things, chickens.'

Brinjolf led them to the group round the game and explained that the visitors were on their way to Nebulo in search of an English queen whose daughter Lily was.

The old men looked at Lily in her boy's clothes with some curiosity but asked no questions. They invited her and the boys to sit with them on the stone seats in the shade.

More old men approached, the frailer among them leaning on stout oak staves. Some wore swords. Helmets, shields, bows and quivers lay on the seats.

When all were sitting in the shade, leaving the game of hnefatfafl unfinished, slaves brought sheepmeat and bitter oranges and poured cool bubbling wine into clay cups.

The boys and Lily had never seen oranges before. Charlotte said she had been eating them for as long as she could remember and that they were 'the love-liest fruit in the world'. She closed her eyes tightly as she squeezed the warm juice down her throat. They were all hungry and thirsty, and all except Charlotte drank the heady wine.

Lily asked Brinjolf where the slaves came from.

'From Kiev,' he said. 'We captured whole families of them before the great defeat, and brought them south with us before the enemy could rescue them. They live in caves. Gloomy folk. You never hear them laugh.'

'Are they kept under guard?'

'No.'

'Why don't they run away?'

'Why would they want to?' Brinjolf said. 'They like it here. As much as they can like anything. It's pleasant enough, after all.'

'For you too?'

'For us too.'

'Don't you want to go home?' Lily asked. She could never understand how anyone could give up his own land.

'Some of us might but none of us can, because we're in disgrace. We call ourselves the Companions in Disgrace.'

'The Cids,' said another old man, 'for short.'

'If we went home,' Brinjolf said, 'it would be to meet our doom.'

'Are you safe here?' Gus asked. 'Won't Vikings come after you here?'

Horsa said, 'Aren't you afraid that *we* might feel in honour bound to kill you?'

All the old warriors laughed at that.

'We feel safe enough with the four of you,' Brinjolf said. 'But we have other enemies in these parts. They spoil things for us a bit. It was only to be expected. Sigvald the Skald, blind seer of the Northlands, prophesied once in Eyiolf's hall that no soldier of his would ever have peace. But we don't mind too much. In a way our enemies are good for us. They give us practice in combat. Keep us on our fighting toes.'

'Who are they?' Mordec asked.

'A horde of Sicilians who fled from a Viking invasion of their island and now attack us for revenge whenever the mood takes them.'

'How often is that?'

'It's hard to say. Every few weeks or every few days. Sometimes we've been attacked twice in a day and then not again for months.'

'Have they killed many of you?' Hengist asked.

'Only a few. They're not well trained or well commanded. Hardly more than a rabble. We always beat them off.'

Now the sun was high and hot. The old men moved to keep in the shade and then most of them fell asleep.

And the heat and the wine had their effect on the boys and Lily. They too fell asleep on stone seats.

the battle

They were woken by three blasts on a trumpet.

'Sichi, Sichi!' they heard a look-out cry, and all round them the stronger of the old men took up their shields, donned their helmets, and scurried with bows and drawn swords to their battle stations.

'Sichi,' Mordec said. 'That must mean Sicilians.'

Horsa drew his sword and led the others to the highest tier. Lying in the grass they caught sight of small dark fellows in the valleys between the near hills scuttling out from behind a rock or tree and into the shadow of another.

Mordec saw that most of the Cids made for the top of the arena and disappeared down the other side. Did that mean, he wondered, that the Sichi usually tried to attack them by coming up the grassy steps?

He went to find out what was happening, followed by Horsa. They lay in the grass so as not to be an easy target for Sichi arrows, and peering over the edge saw why the Cids made for the stairs. They used the big stones as shields.

'But why go down at all?' Hengist said. 'They can best defend this place from above—it's a natural fortress.'

Horsa pointed to the valley. 'Look, that's why!'

A stream of Cids were chasing a jostle of Sichi, swords in hand and with terrific hullabaloo, the chasers yelling and the chased squealing.

'So they like to go over at once to the attack,' Horsa said.

'They should fan out,' Gus said, crawling up behind them.

'No because—there, you can see now why not,' Horsa said, pointing again.

Some of the Sichi turned, aimed their bows and shot a concentrated rain of arrows at their pursuers. But the Cids raised their shields to form a roof, and warded them off. The chase went on.

'Let's go,' Horsa said, and started scrambling down the grassy steps.

'Yes!' Gus shouted, leaping recklessly and overtaking him.

'What if the Sichi turn and attack us?' Hengist asked. 'I mean, none of us have armour on.'

'I think,' Mordec said, 'that they don't do that.'

A small voice called out near by, 'A dance, a dance!' It was Charlotte, jumping with excitement as she watched the battle.

'She's right,' Mordec said, laughing.

'Anyway, let's go,' Hengist said, starting off after the others.

'Coming?' Mordec asked Lily.

She shook her head. 'It's not my fight.' Staying where she was she kept her eyes on Gus, who had reached the valley and was running hard to overtake the old men.

By the time Mordec and Hengist were down the hill, Gus and Horsa had overtaken the Cids and were gaining on the Sichi, brandishing their swords and emitting bird-shrieks shriller than the wordless war-cries of the lumbering old warriors or their flitting enemies.

Lily saw Gus drive off two Sichi before the battle moved out of sight round the next hill. Then only the yells told her that it was still going on. Later Gus told her he had beaten six of them in close combat, and she believed him. Horsa was to say that he'd wounded one before they scattered into the hills.

By the time Mordec and Hengist reached the spot where hand-to-hand fighting had briefly taken place, not a Sichi was in sight except on the ground, where lay two dead and three wounded.

Brinjolf stood over one of the corpses looking him over attentively.

'Not exactly a youngster,' he said. 'Couldn't run as he used to do.'

He drew an axe from his belt, put a foot on the dead man's chest and cut off the head with two blows.

Holding it up by the hair he told Mordec, 'I've been after this one for years. Now I'll make his skull my drinking cup.'

'Look,' Hengist shouted. 'There are some over there, among the trees.'

He pointed, and three Sichi broke cover and sprinted over a stretch of grass and sand. In the wink of an eye Hengist and Mordec were after them.

'Youth!' Brinjolf sighed enviously. 'How it can run!'

Mordec outstripped Hengist and coming in between two of the Sichi laid about him with his sword, swinging it blindly left and right. He felt it strike once, twice, three times, and the Sichi shrieked and clutched themselves, one his head, the other a shoulder.

Both ran on, the man with the headwound staggering behind the other through a stream.

The third was Hengist's quarry and had almost escaped his pursuer when Hengist took out his dagger, held it by the blade and sent it spinning through the air at the back of the fleeing man, which it hit but only grazed. The man yelped and ran faster, splashed through the water and started up the hill on the other side.

At the streamside Mordec and Hengist stopped. They could see the danger, clusters of rocks where the enemy could be crouching. Weapons in hand they stepped cautiously back, watching for a sudden attack.

And it came. Arrows sang through the air straight at them. Mordec put an arm across his face to protect his glasses from a shattering arrow, and at the same time he dropped into the grass.

Hengist dropped too, and fell on a sharp stone. He cried out as it gashed his lips.

Mordec turned and saw the blood. As it was gushing from Hengist's mouth, he thought the wound must be in his neck or chest. 'I must bind it fast,' he thought.

Hoping that no missiles would come speeding towards them in the next half minute, he rose, seized

Hengist under the arms and began to drag him across the open stretch of grass and sand towards the shelter of rocks and shadow.

Arrows sang. He fell on top of Hengist, wishing he had a helmet and shield.

The arrows hit the ground less than two feet from where they lay.

Picturing the little men fitting more arrows to bowstrings, he seized Hengist again and as he dragged him panted out, 'Hang on Hengist—don't die—we're nearly there!'

They reached shelter before more arrows came singing through the air and thumping into the ground no nearer to them than the last time.

Mordec cut his sleeve and ripped off a long strip of it. Then he looked for Hengist's wound. The neck was so bathed in blood there was no telling where the cut might be. Hengist tried to say something, but his lips were swelling so he couldn't shape the words. Mordec bent an ear close to the bleeding mouth, thinking that his friend might be trying to groan out his last words.

'Ny nips,' he heard. 'It's only ny nips.' And after a moment or two Mordec understood.

'Your lips,' he said. 'Only your lips have been cut?'

Hengist nodded.

'Well, I can't bind them up unless I gag you,' Mordec said, sounding cross out of sheer relief. And then the same feeling made him laugh.

'It's not nunny!' Hengist said, getting to his feet and putting a hand over the bleeding side of his mouth.

Just then Gus and Horsa came creeping round the hillside looking for them.

'What happened?' Gus asked when he saw Hengist's face. 'You've been wounded!'

'A stone,' Hengist managed to utter.

'Stones? They were using stones?'

'I fell on a stone.'

'Oh, you fell! Still, it's a wound,' Gus said. 'I envy you!'

'I ish I could gi it to you,' Hengist said, struggling with his tongue at the back of his throat.

They moved cautiously until they had rounded the hill and were back where the Cids stood among the wounded and the dead. Brinjolf cheered when he saw them.

Again Hengist gave the briefest explanation of how he'd come by his wound. Whether or not they'd understood, the Cids cheered again.

'We're glad that young Vikings can fight as bravely today as we could at your age,' Brinjolf said. 'Come back to the theatre and we'll drink to the heroic life you four will live following in our footsteps.'

Gus looked glum. 'Their footsteps! They were never heroes,' he muttered to Mordec. 'Have they forgotten they're in disgrace? Why are you smiling? You're always finding things funny when they're not.'

'I'm smiling for the reasons you just gave,' Mordec said. 'The Companions in Disgrace telling us we'll be good like them.'

'And that's funny? I don't understand you,' Gus said. 'I don't think I'll ever understand you.'

sam's law

That night the boys devoured bread and chicken ravenously, though Hengist had difficulty poking food into his swollen mouth. They tried not to join in the drinking which went on for hours with many a song of battle, slaughter, and victory.

The Cids pressed them to fill their cups but they shook their heads. Mordec tried to explain that they must start early for Nebulo and the wine would make them sleep too soundly and too long but the old men seemed not to be listening. And when Brinjolf stood before them with a brimming horn and told them that it was 'the sacred vessel' and that he had brought it to them 'as it is always brought to warriors who have fought the most bravely' and that it would be outraging a time-honoured custom if they didn't drink from it, they felt they had no choice. One by one they took it and drank, though none of them could remember ever having heard of such a custom.

When they woke the next day the sun was high, their heads felt heavy, they were bound hand and foot, and their weapons and bags were nowhere in sight.

Nor was Lily.

Helping each other they soon freed themselves from their bonds, and then Mordec found that his gold was gone too. They had been robbed of everything except the clothes they had on and—to Mordec's unspoken relief—his glasses.

'What's happened? Where's Lily?' Gus said.

'Where are the Cids?' Mordec said. 'They've all gone. They haven't even left a look-out.'

'Hullo-o-o!' Gus called.

Silence.

'Lilee-ee-ee!'

Silence.

'They must have taken her somewhere. But where? Why? I'll go to the top and see if I can see them out there.'

The others watched Gus go.

'Something weird's going on,' Mordec said.

'Maybe the Black Monks came while we were asleep,' Horsa said. 'Maybe they came with the Army of the Redeemed and took her away.'

'Why her and not us?' Mordec said. 'Or you at least. I thought it was you they wanted?'

'You're right! They would have taken me. Or all four of us. And anyway, if a whole army had come the racket would've woken us.' Horsa paced about for a minute or two pondering the mystery. Then he asked, 'Could the Sichi have come while the Cids were all away somewhere and robbed us and taken Lily?'

'The Sichi would've killed us for sure,' Mordec said.

Gus came back and reported that there was no one in sight. 'They're all gone, and they must have taken her with them.'

'Who? The Cids?' Horsa felt bewildered, or still dazed by the wine.

'Yes. And they robbed us,' Mordec said.

'But why would they do that—after we'd fought beside them?' Horsa asked.

'They say themselves that they're not men of honour,' Mordec reminded him.

'Do you suppose,' Gus said, angry and scornful, 'that men who slaughtered thousands of their own folk as carelessly as if they were sheep just because Eyiolf told them to, and then didn't even have the decency to die when the rest of Eyiolf's army was cut down, would hold back from killing us four just because we're Vikings?'

Hengist, even less able to speak now through lips puffed and scabbed, groaned his agreement.

'All that nonsense with the so-called sacred drinking horn,' Mordec said, full of irritation with himself for having believed it. 'We fell for it like daft fools! They drugged us so they could rob us.'

'So they could take Lily,' Gus said. 'But why? Why Lily?'

'And why leave us alive, and here, to face them with what they've done when they return?'

'I think they meant us to run off. They might've thought that when we found ourselves without weapons we'd want to get away.'

'It's all very mysterious,' Mordec said.

Gus was becoming impatient. 'We've just got to find her,' he said.

'Where? How? What do we do now?' Horsa asked.

'They'll have to come back here,' Mordec said. 'This is where they live. We'll just wait.'

'Yes,' Gus agreed. 'And if they don't bring Lily back we'll have to make them tell us where she is.'

'And why they took her away,' Mordec said.

'Wherever she is I'll find her,' Gus said. 'As long as I'm alive I'll never give up looking for her.'

Hengist and Horsa looked at him with surprise. 'Why not?' Horsa said.

Gus's face started to redden but he was saved from answering by Mordec who reminded them that the whole point of their quest was to help Lily find her mother, and that if she wasn't with them there was no point in their going on. '*We* have no use for Queen Gloria,' he said. 'Quite the opposite.'

'But we can't just let them take Lily and do nothing,' Gus said. 'I mean it wouldn't be—'

'Honourable?' Horsa asked.

'It would mean a waste of all this time and effort,' Mordec said.

'So you'll help me find her?' Gus asked, turning to him eagerly.

'Of course,' Mordec said, to Gus's obvious relief.

But as Mordec met Gus's anxious gaze he slowly closed one eyelid and opened it again. Gus's face turned fiery red. He covered his confusion with sudden resolution. 'I don't think we should just sit around here waiting. Let's go and look for her. Come on. They can't have taken her far.'

Mordec was struck by a new idea. 'Maybe they're hiding underground,' he suggested.

They looked at each other. To search down there they'd have to descend in single file—easy targets to pick off one by one.

'We'll have to go and look,' Gus said. 'If that's where they are, that's where they may be holding Lily. I'll go first. Stand close and be ready to haul me out fast if they attack.'

They stood round the opening and Gus stepped down, slowly at first, peering into the dimness below, then he quickened his steps and the others followed.

For a few moments they stood at the bottom of the stairs unable to make out anything much, but soon they could see well enough. They looked into storerooms where staves and straw, skittles and balls were kept, and the parts and pieces for boardgames.

'They must have a secret place for weapons and armour,' Horsa said.

'Here's a bolted door,' Mordec called. 'The bolt's stiff—come and give me a hand. There, that's it. Odds-bods! Look at this.'

Not weapons and armour but clothes filled the shelves, stacks of them piled to the roof.

Mordec pulled some garments down and unfolded them. 'Women's clothes!'

'Women's clothes!' Gus repeated in a tone of horror.

'We never thought why they have no wives. They must capture women and then murder them and keep their clothes.'

'The question is,' Mordec said, 'what do they want the clothes for?'

'Whatever they want them for, they want them. We can see that.'

'Lily wasn't wearing women's clothes,' Horsa reminded them.

'No, she wasn't, you're right! Then why have they taken her?'

'We'll wait and ask them,' Mordec said.

'We'll go and look for Lily,' said Gus. 'Come on.'

'Where can we begin?' Horsa wondered aloud, looking about him when they stood in the open air again.

Gus led them up the tiers of seats. As soon as he reached the top he dropped into the grass. 'Down!' he hissed. They lay flat and peered over. Twenty Cids were advancing, in ranks of two, all bent under a roof of shields, swords in hand.

'What are they doing?' Mordec whispered. 'They can't be coming after us. If they wanted us dead they could have killed us in our sleep.'

'I think they're just exercising,' Horsa said. 'Practicing battle formation for attack.'

'They're cowardly old brutes,' Gus said. 'I think we should kill some of them. We'd only be doing our duty if we did.'

'With what?' Horsa said. 'Kill them with what?'

Hengist began to make excited noises. They looked at him but couldn't make out what he was trying to tell them. He stepped down among the seats to a place where no grass grew and beckoned to the others excitedly. When they came to stand beside him he pushed them back, swept a hand over the sandy patch and began drawing with his finger, grunting and sometimes pointing. Mordec was the first to understand.

'He's saying something about those walls with the big round stones on them. He's saying—yes, yes I see. What Sam showed us? That's how you mean we should? Right.'

'What's he getting at?' Gus asked impatiently.

'We'll show you. Come on Hengist, let's try it.'

When Gus and Horsa understood what Hengist and Mordec had in mind they all got busy.

They fetched strong oak staves and took them to the top of the grass-covered stairway where they lay low in the grass. Hengist selected two of the staves for Gus and Mordec. Slithering on their bellies, they dragged themselves over the edge. They rose only when they were close enough to the first pair of great round stones to be wholly hidden from anyone looking up from below.

They wedged the staves as far as they'd go under the two top stones so that they stuck up at an angle from the ground. Mordec and Gus took each a firm grip on his lever.

As they couldn't see what was happening below, they kept their eyes fixed on Hengist and Horsa who kept watch from the grass above. The signal was to be the clapping of their hands above their heads, Hengist for Mordec, Horsa for Gus.

Mordec flexed his muscles as he pressed experimentally on his oak staff, suddenly doubting that it would prove strong enough after all.

But it was. The stone rocked slightly. Then Mordec wondered if he himself had the strength to lever the stone all the way off its ledge. He wouldn't know for sure until the moment came for the stone to start rolling. The Cids seemed to be taking an age to cover a few hundred yards. Mordec's breath came shorter and faster as the wait went on.

Hengist clapped his hands and Mordec fell on his lever, pressed his whole body on to it with all his might and felt the stone begin to move.

So absorbed was he in his task he didn't hear Horsa's signal for Gus which was given a moment later. But he was aware of Hengist suddenly standing beside him and adding his own weight and strength to the pressure. Together they dislodged the great stone and sent it rolling against the next one which it struck with a loud clonk. A double clonk they heard, for Horsa and Gus had set their stone in motion too. They lay heads down and listened, holding their breath, and 'Clonk-clonk,' they heard, 'clonk-clonk, clonk-clonk,'—four times, five times, and then a cho-rus-shout of surprise, outrage—and pain perhaps.

'Quick!' Gus said. They scrambled to the top, ran round to the other side of the hill, and began to leap down the slope, but stopped half-way. Cids had come round the hill and were climbing towards them, mov-ing not quickly but steadily.

The boys turned their head and looked up.

More of the old warriors were coming over the top and descending on them, swords in hand. In another moment they would seize and overpower the unarmed boys.

But just then a trumpet sounded, three loud blasts.

'Sichi! Sichi!' the cry went up, and the old Vikings scattered, shrieking, to their posts.

The way was clear for the boys to make their escape. They bounded to the bottom and made for the nearest cover, a mound of rocks overshadowed by saplings, and from there hurried round the next hill.

There they stayed, lying in the grass and recovering their breath, content enough to remain patient and still for an hour or even more, though they hoped to be able to start their search for Lily before the sun went down.

The war-cries stopped. No sounds of battle reached them. They heard no footstep approaching, saw no moving shadow on the grass, felt no presence, and none of them suspected that any living thing larger than an insect could be within a hundred yards of them, but on to Gus's back jumped a creature with a distinctly human and mischievous laugh.

Gus grunted as the breath was knocked out of him, and the others shot up, fear and surprise on their faces, which only made the creature laugh more. Their expressions changed to a mixture of relief and irritation when they saw that it was only Charlotte who had silently crept up on them. They had forgotten all about Charlotte. Gus pushed her roughly off his back and she half-lay in the grass, her head propped on one hand while the other waved something about which glinted in the sinking light of the sun. A trumpet. Understanding dawned on them.

'You blew the trumpet?' Mordec said.

Charlotte nodded and laughed.

'You made the Cids believe Sichi were attacking? So we could run and save ourselves?'

More nods and giggles. The little dancer was obviously feeling very pleased with herself.

'How did you get the trumpet?' Gus demanded.

'I went and danced for the dark people last night. They live in little stone houses but they all cook on one fire. After I'd danced for them they gave me amber beads and small coins and a kitten. You look funny,' she said to Hengist.

'What have you done with the coins?' Mordec asked.

'I'm *telling* you. I came to find you but you were all asleep and I couldn't wake you. So I went back to the dark people and asked them for a trumpet. And they gave me this. But they took back the beads and the coins and the kitten. Then I slept near the fire and came back in the morning to find you. I saw two big stone balls falling off the hill.'

'Did they hit anyone?' Mordec asked, and Hengist made noises which were probably meant to be the same question.

'No. But I think the old men got a big surprise. They heard the stones banging together and they looked up and saw them moving and then the bottom ones falling off. I think they were a bit cross about it. Was it you made the stones roll down? I couldn't see you anywhere. I walked right round the hill, and then I saw you coming over the top and I wanted you to wait for me.'

'So that's why you blew the trumpet?'

Charlotte nodded.

'Well, it was lucky you did,' Gus said. 'I don't s'pose you know where Lily is?'

Charlotte nodded again.

the princess starling

'We're back on the road to Brevis, anyway,' Mordec said. 'But how do you know that Lily is somewhere along this way?'

'I saw them take her,' Charlotte said. 'I saw them put her in a wagon and take her this way.'

'But when did you see this?'

'When I was coming back after dancing for the dark little people. That's why I tried to wake you up.'

'But who took her? How?'

'I *told* you, the old men put her in a *wagon*,' Charlotte said, impatiently spreading out her hands as though she'd told them this many times and they just wouldn't listen. 'And the *wagon* was going this way. And then I came to fetch you but you were asleep and I couldn't wake you up. So I went for the trumpet.'

'That was very clever of you,' Mordec said.

'But I *am* clever, I keep *telling* you.'

Mordec hadn't heard Charlotte saying so but it wasn't a point worth arguing about. The light was fading and he was thinking that they must find a place to hide until daylight. If they were set upon in the night by robbers or slavers they would find it hard to defend themselves without weapons. Horsa had been thinking much the same thing. 'We'd better stop now and wait for first light,' he said.

'No, not yet,' Gus said. 'It's not dark yet. Let's go on for another mile or two.'

So they trudged on through the dusk, and had passed two milestones when Charlotte stopped, pointed, and said 'Look! There! The lights and the fire.'

'How d'you know the wagon will be there?' Gus said.

Because there were *lots* of wagons and they'd have to stop somewhere, wouldn't they?'

'Lots of wagons? You just said "a wagon".'

'I said they put Lily into a wagon,' Charlotte said impatiently. 'But that wagon was with lots of other wagons.'

'Come on then,' Gus said, and began to run, so the others ran to keep up with him.

'She's right, there *are* lots of them,' Mordec said. 'Look—huge things.'

'Covered over, and with lanterns burning inside them,' Horsa said.

The many, huge, covered wagons were drawn into a circle on a large stretch of flat grassland beside the road. No guards were to be seen. The boys crept close then lay down and peered between wheels to see what was going on in the middle of the circle. A fire was burning. Horses were grazing. And men dressed like the Moorish captain in full trousers and with scimitars in their sashes were carrying platters of food from the fire to the wagons.

Gus grabbed Charlotte's arm and pulled her back some yards before he whispered, 'Where is she?'

'*In* a wagon,' Charlotte said, again spreading her hands.

'But which one? Which one did they put her into?'

'The one with the *green* cover. I told you.'

'You didn't,' Gus said.

'I *did,* only none of you ever *listens* to me,'

That can't be true, Gus thought, but he had no time to argue about it now.

'Where is the one with the green cover?'

'Over there.' She pointed.

'What's over there?' Mordec asked.

'The wagon they took Lily in,' Charlotte said. Then she shook her head. 'I don't know how you'd manage without me.' She sounded so much like a little old lady exasperated by their stupidity that Mordec laughed.

'Let's go,' Gus said.

They turned, but found two men blocking their way, each holding a scimitar in one hand and letting the flat of the blade lie on his other palm. Together in perfect unison they raised their weapons and pointed with them to show their captives where to go. There was no sense in trying to run away. Meekly the boys obeyed and the men followed them.

Nobody noticed Charlotte slipping away among the wheels.

The boys were led round the outside of the circle until they came to the green-covered wagon. At its rear was a short ladder. They went up, pushed through a gauzy curtain and found themselves looking down at a number of seated women.

Lily was not among them.

Mordec glanced behind him and saw the guards standing before the curtain, their blades laid on their palms.

He turned back to survey the company.

On carpets of many colours and patterns the women sat cross-legged. They too were dressed in full trousers and wide sashes. Their faces were covered from the noses down. They wore jewels in their hair and on their fingers, and their short jackets glittered in the lantern-light with jewels or glass or threads of gold. Some held musical instruments.

Mordec's eyes moved over them and stopped at a figure reclining on silk cushions at the far end; a large woman, the largest he had ever seen. Her veil and garments shimmered green and blue. She had bushy eyebrows and a headful of oiled blue-black curls sprinkled with sparkling ornaments.

Gazing languidly at the boys she spoke words the boys could not understand in a deep voice.

A heavy curtain opened behind her and in came a short wiry man, wizened though not old, dressed like a northerner in buckskins. The woman spoke again and he after her, translating her words. Her speech rose and fell with feeling, but her interpreter spoke woodenly.

'What beautiful fair hair you have,' he said staring into the air. 'And how tall and young and handsome you are. Also I see two others. But one is ugly. He has a very ugly mouth. Put him out.'

Before the man had finished speaking, the two guards had seized Hengist and pushed him through the gauze curtain and down the steps.

Mordec looked at the man. 'Are you from England?' he asked.

The man said something in the lady's language, presumably translating Mordec's question.

She spoke again, then the man again. But Mordec's question was left unanswered.

'I'm very glad to see you are so tall and young and handsome and I know why you have come.'

'We've come to find someone,' Gus said. 'A friend of ours. Her name is Lily.'

'Lily Queen of the Fenreach,' the lady herself said.

'Yes. So you know who I'm talking about?'

'I do.' The interpreter said. 'She is here. I am taking her to England with me as I was paid to do. I am treating her well. She is bound with cords of silk. She eats the food I eat and drinks my golden wine and I bestow on her the heroic dreams of heavenly hashish.'

'What's that?' Gus asked suspiciously, and got no answer.

'Who paid you to take her?' Mordec asked.

'The Companions in Disgrace paid with gold.'

'Gold coins?' Mordec asked. 'May I see one of them?'

The lady nodded and waved a hand and one of the girls went to a chest, unlocked it, took out one gold coin and brought it to Mordec, holding it up in front of his eyes. When he tried to take hold of it and look at it more closely she pulled it away, then held it up again. Keeping his hands at his sides this time Mordec peered at the coin.

As he'd suspected, it was from Eyiolf's hoard. Of course the Cids *might* have such coins themselves, but Mordec doubted it. He guessed that the Cids had used his money, or some of it, to bribe this lady to take Lily back to England bound and drugged. But why? Who was behind the plot? Who wanted Lily gone but not harmed? Not the Cids themselves, surely. They could have sold her into slavery. Someone must have given them orders which they dared not disobey, and the question was, who could that someone be?

'That coin was stolen from *me* by the Companions in Disgrace,' he said.

'Guard your money better next time.' The interpreter said it flatly, but the lady giggled, delighted with her teasing.

'Do you want to know who we are?' Mordec asked.

'I know who you are.'

'Are you going to hold us prisoner?'

'No.'

'Will you tell us who *you* are?'

'I am the Princess Starling. I come from Baghdad. My father turned all my lovers away and even kept their names secret from me. But I have a right to a husband, I told him, I have a right. Then I made him give me gold and slaves and guards to travel to

England, because my interpreter told me that I'd be sure to find a husband there. I will make a wonderful wife to a good man! I live to love. I'm a sensitive person. Feeling is all that matters to me. And a girl is only young and beautiful for a short time so she must find a husband while the bloom is on her.'

When her interpreter had finished saying these words the Princess sat up straight and removed the veil from the lower part of her face. She had several chins and a fluffy ginger moustache.

'Come, sit and eat and drink,' she said graciously. 'I love to have beautiful people round me, and you boys are beautiful.'

As if with one voice the boys—who'd learnt not to consume anything freely given by the hand of a stranger—replied that they were not hungry or thirsty.

'Well, dear boys, I won't take offense. The ways of your people are different from the ways of my people. But if I can't persuade you to eat and drink with me then you must choose between two fates which I decree.'

The boys stiffened as they waited for the dooms to be named. Another hole they'd got themselves into! What was it to be this time—death or slavery?

'You can stay with me forever or you can run into the night. Choose.'

the floating town

They slept in long grass and by luck neither men nor beasts came upon them. When they woke day had dawned.

Gus climbed a hill to look for the wagons of the Princess Starling, but they'd gone.

'What now?' Horsa said. 'I'm hungry.'

'Me too,' Hengist managed to say, his lips being less swollen this morning.

'We must get to Brevis,' Mordec said, standing up and stretching. 'My grandfather will give us whatever we need.'

'But we can't just let Lily go—if we don't follow the trail of those wagons now we'll lose them,' Gus protested.

'We can't go looking for her without food or money or weapons,' Mordec said reasonably. 'Come on, we've not far to go. And we may even catch up with the wagons in the city.'

This persuaded Gus, so they started off. In less than two hours they saw the town. As they descended a mountainside and looked over a wide valley, there it was, blue walls encircling more blue walls, flecks of gold on a tower or two, and all seeming to float on a cushion of mist.

Mordec's heart beat faster as he thought that soon he would see his grandfather again. He had only one memory of him from more than ten years earlier, when the finely clothed man wearing glasses in front of his eyes, the man who was his mother's father had stood in their house and bent over a small Mordec to give him his first pair of eyeglasses and a book about Alexander the Conqueror. 'I brought these in case your eyes were like mine, bad at seeing anything far away, and I can tell they are,' he'd said. 'And I brought you this because—but you will know when you read it.'

Mordec hurried ahead of the others. Traffic thickened as they approached the town and at a crossroads near the walls there was quite a crush. The gates stood open in a blue arch on which GAUDIUM BREVIS was written in gilded letters. Mordec read the words aloud to the others and wondered what they meant.

Within the arch, travellers and traders sat on ledges as wide as benches, resting or bargaining. Among them Lily lolled, her back against the wall, arms folded on her chest, cap pulled forward over her eyes, and beside her sat Charlotte swinging her legs. When the dancer saw the boys and their surprised looks, she laughed and shook Lily roughly.

'They're here, wake up, they're here.'

Lily pushed her cap off her face, stared at the boys for a moment, and then smiled. Gus said, 'You're safe!'

The six of them stood in the arch, in everybody's way, knocked by porters, shouted at by drovers, while the boys heard through the babble of voices and the creaking of wheels and the snort of horses how Lily, on finally waking before dawn from her long sleep and 'amazing dreams of being crowned Queen of all England in a castle just like Sec-et-Doux', had been released from bonds of silk and a prison of gauze. It was the interpreter who'd set her free.

'Though I could easily have got those cords off by myself,' she said, 'once I was fully awake.'

She'd found Charlotte asleep in the grass near by, wet with dew.

They moved into the town.

'Why d'you think he let you go, the interpreter?' Gus asked Lily.

'He said the Princess wouldn't mind, she had the gold the Cids had paid her and that would be enough for her. He said she's kind and lazy, and didn't really want to be bothered with me. She told him more than once that royal hostages are a nuisance at the best of times and a headache when you're on the road.'

'Did she know he was setting you free?'

'No. But he said she wouldn't punish him for it.'

'Did he say if they'd paid her a lot?' Mordec asked.

'They must have because she didn't want to do it. I heard her say it wouldn't be very good for her to be known in England as someone who'd held an English queen captive. I wanted to tell her she was right, I'd hunt her down myself. But I felt too sleepy to say anything.'

'*I'd* have hunted her down,' Gus said, 'long before she got to England.'

'The interpreter advised her to go there to find a husband because he wanted to go home. He said he'd have married her himself if necessary but luckily she wanted somebody younger and handsomer.'

Lily laughed as she told them this, and Mordec laughed too. Even Horsa smiled, and Hengist might have if he'd been able to. But Gus, as usual, couldn't see the joke.

In the market-place Mordec approached the first rich-looking merchant he saw and asked him if he could direct them to the house of Adam son of Mordecai.

'And who may you be who seeks him?' the merchant asked, looking round for the boys' wagons.

'His grandson from the North,' Mordec said.

'Ah,' said the merchant, and gave them directions.

When Mordec knocked on his grandfather's front door he noticed that the blue buildings of which the whole city consisted were made in a different way from any others he had ever seen. Hengist too had noticed this. He ran his hand over the surface of stiff blue woven material and felt how it held together a hard structure underneath, sets of blocks of stone or clay in rows and stacks.

'Hmm, clever. Quick and easy to build,' Hengist remarked.

At that moment the door was opened by a man-servant in blue livery who gaped in disbelief when Mordec said he was 'the grandson from the North'.

'Wait here,' the servant said severely, and shut the door. It opened again and Adam son of Mordecai himself stood on the threshold. He had less hair than when Mordec had seen him last, and what there was of it was white. And of course he didn't seem as tall now that Mordec looked down instead of up into his grandfather's eyes. Two pairs of eyeglasses inspected each other.

For a few moments Grandfather Adam had to search the young man's face to find the boy he remembered. But when he found it he gave him and all of them as hearty a welcome as Mordec could have hoped for.

They devoured a very large breakfast while they told Adam the purpose and events of their present journey as well as last year's adventures in England.

He listened with attention and sympathy. Then he had questions to ask about his daughter in the North, about Hauk, their honey and meadmaking business, and more than were necessary in Mordec's opinion about the baby Eyrin.

Now for the first time Mordec learnt how he'd come by his name. His full name, Adam said, was 'Matthew Mordecai, after my father Mordecai and his father Matthew. But your mother and father wanted you to have a name that wouldn't sound too strange in the Northlands, so they shortened it to Mordec.'

'It still sounds strange,' Gus said.

Mordec, Adam and Lily laughed.

'Have I said something funny?'

Adam patted Gus's arm. 'Stay here with me, all of you, as long as you can,' he said.

'We can't stay,' Lily reminded him, 'because we have to find my mother.'

'Well, when you've found her bring her to Brevis. If Brevis is still here.'

'Why wouldn't it be?' Mordec asked.

'It's a moveable town,' Adam said, 'and it might have to be moved again soon. Have you seen how it's built? It can be taken apart quickly and put together again somewhere else. We've moved it more than once and we'd do it again. But we'd be sorry to go from here. It's a good place. We'll only go if we must.'

'But why would you have to?'

'We Lombards are not liked and we're often set upon by mobs and armed bands. And now there's a new threat—the Army of the Redeemed. It's a growing band of ruffians recruited and armed by the order which the Black Monks belong to. And their plan has the blessing of the Pope.'

'We've heard of it. And the Black Monks on Sam's island were scary,' Horsa said feelingly, 'especially the Abbot.'

'They've threatened us more than once. They hate us because we sell money rather than grain or cloth or horses. They need what we sell, mind you, but that makes no difference. Sometimes I think they hate us all the more *because* they need us. We've asked all the bishops in the Valley of the Po to protect us, and they say they will. There are good men among them but they have no armies. And then there are some who're in our debt and wouldn't mind if someone else got rid of us. So what we need is a fighting force. Not a large one. A hundred trained soldiers would do if they were well led.'

Adam showed them round the town. On the public buildings a motto was written in gold: *'Gaudium Longum Non Est'.*

'It means,' Adam said, 'that there is no lasting happiness. And that's why we call our town Gaudium Brevis which means Brief Joy.'

The biggest building stood beside the busy market place. 'It's called a hospital. People who are sick go there and physicians try to cure them, and quite often they do. And women who are skilled at cooling fevers and warming chills bathe and feed and soothe them.'

'We should have hospitals in the North,' Mordec said.

'And in England,' Lily said.

'Yes, and then I'd dance for the sick people,' Charlotte said, 'and you would pay me, wouldn't you?'

'I would. And if you stay,' Adam told his grandson, 'you can learn to be a physician. Or study Law. There's a school of Lombard Law not far from here at Pavia.'

He gave them clothes, boots, woolen cloaks, full-length swords, daggers, armour, and bags full of useful things. He had gold coins sewn into the hem of Mordec's tunic, and hung a purse of silver round his neck. 'And if you need more, take this paper' he said, 'to the Lombard whose name is on it and whose house is in the Concourse of the Martyrs in Nebulo and he will give you what you need. Though I don't think he'll have enough to pay a ransom for Queen Gloria. If it's a ransom they want, they must give us time to raise it.'

'We couldn't repay such a debt,' Lily said. 'I gave our gold to the Vikings to help set Mordec free.'

'Then I owe it to you,' Adam replied. 'Now I've found out the safest way for you to travel from here to Nebulo—with a great procession of the church. The Pope is making a "progress" all the way up Italy from Rome to the Alps, and you will join it.'

'Why is he doing it?' Lily asked.

'They say it's for him to give charity to the poor. That the poor cannot come to Rome for it because of the constant wars in the city. The story has some truth in it. There *are* constant wars in Rome between the Pope's men and the Emperor's men. Lately the Emperor threatened to kill the Pope so the Pope wanted an excuse to get out of the city without giving up his throne. That's the real reason for the progress. It's a shrewd move. As he travels his following gets bigger. Every day more men, women and children join his train. With them you'll be safe from the Army of the Redeemed, and guarded from criminal bands. But still watch your things carefully. The Pope's guards themselves are not above robbery.'

'Will they let pagans like us go with them?' Gus asked.

'Don't tell anyone you are pagans,' Adam warned him. 'The spirit of the times is against you.'

'We could've worn our crosses,' Mordec said, 'the ones Djil gave us, if the Cids hadn't stolen them with all our other things.'

'Crosses,' Adam said. 'That's the right idea. You'll have them. Big wooden crosses to hang round your necks. I'll order five.'

'One for me too,' Charlotte said.

'Six crosses.'

'Not for me,' Horsa said. 'I'll stay here. I'll teach anyone who wants to learn how to use a sword. Or a scimitar. And if the Army of the Redeemed attack, I'll be happy to help defend this town.' Brief though happiness might be, the joy of armed combat made life worth living, and a chance of defeating the forces of the Black Monks was well worth waiting for.

Adam smiled. 'Good,' he said. 'That's one soldier for us. We need ninety-nine more like you. And only five crosses.'

'Four,' Hengist said. 'I'll also stay here a while. It's a good place to make new weapons.'

'What new weapons do you have in mind?'

Hengist told him about an idea he had for putting Sam's Law to deadly use, and Adam got some other Lombards to come and hear about it too. 'If you have a row of small iron balls in a pipe,' Hengist explained, 'and you knock them at one end with one ball, very hard, the ball at the other end will shoot out with the same force. If it's fast enough it will wound a man, perhaps even kill him. I've got to try out ways of making it shoot out fast enough. Of course, if you could send a single ball all the way through on its own with enough speed it would do the same thing, but I haven't thought how to do that.'

One of the Lombards asked him if he could make a weapon which would strike many of the enemy at the same time. Hengist thought about it for a few moments and said he'd like to try.

progress

So only Mordec, Gus, Lily and Charlotte joined the Great Progress. It would not enter Brevis, Adam told them, since no one in this town was listed for the Pope's charity, and that was not surprising as no one who lived there needed it.

They waited at the crossroads near the gates, Adam, Horsa and Hengist with them, and a crowd of other folk. The procession approached in a cloud of dust that filled the valley and blotted out the sky. It took hours to pass and was a wonderful sight.

The Pope himself, a boy of seventeen with pale curled hair and a wet loose mouth, rode on an elephant, clothed in white and seated on a golden chair under a white canopy. Behind him came hundreds of nobles and high church dignitaries on caparisoned horses, each followed by a servant with a bucket and spade to scoop up the horse-droppings which they sold to peasants as 'blessed manure'. The guards wore golden helmets, golden breastplates and golden buckles on their shoes, full trousers striped in scarlet and gold, carrying pikes ribboned with the same colours, and marching to the beat of fifty small drums hung from the necks of fifty boy drummers. There were trumpeters too, and Charlotte went at once with her trumpet to march among them and blow the tunes they blew as best she could.

Next came the Black Monks walking on bare bloodstained feet, a thousand in all, hoods over bent heads, hands clasped together in the gesture of prayer, heavy crosses hanging on ropes from their waists. As they went by, Horsa stood well back in the crowd.

Then came the long straggle of village priests, towns-folk, and the poor, together called 'the holy penitents', all hoping to be led to heaven. Ten thousand or more there were, some well-fed and some hungry, some handsomely clothed, many in tatters. The hungry begged from the watchers as they went by, and the people of Brevis showered them with coins.

Mordec, Gus and Lily entered the long train of followers near the tail end, bearing their bags—and wearing their crosses. Lily was dressed in boy's clothes as usual, the cap hiding her hair. Five hours later they reached a city on the outskirts of which the procession remained for a week and a day, because the progress was held up by a dispute between the Pope's clerks and the city's Official Poor.

The complaint of the Official Poor was that the fees they were paid for filling this position were not enough. Not only was the price of everything going up, but ten percent of the ten percent which the local church was supposed to pay them was now being diverted for the Army of the Redeemed. They could no longer keep their houses in the poor quarter looking ramshackle and pitiful on the pittance they received, they said.

'Ramshackle and pitiful,' their spokeswoman pointed out, 'don't come cheap.'

This lady had been born with a mournful face which proved to be her fortune. It marked her out for selection by the Bishop to be one of the Official Poor, provided that she married and bore many children, and provided that her husband and children properly performed their 'poor-duties'. She and her family had done all that was wanted of them, until now. Mordec, Gus and Lily saw her coming and going from the Bishop's house several times a day while the negotiations were underway. She wore sad-looking garments made of scratchy sackcloth—though rumor had it they were lined with silk.

The dispute was settled eventually. Then, before an audience of thousands, the city's Official Poor—three large families—knelt in a row in the cathedral square. The Pope's chair, carried on the shoulders of ten Black Monks, was set down before them. He stepped out and walked along their line, stopping before each of them and dipping his hand into a casket which the Bishop, walking beside him, carried on a cushion. Into the outstretched, begging hands of husbands, wives and children, the Pope dropped small coins, specially minted for this purpose. Then the Pope was carried off again in his chair, the Bishop went back into his palace with his casket and cushion, and the Great Progress formed up in procession and started for the next town and the next alms-giving.

At night the nobles and dignitaries of the Church lodged in castles, the guards in colourful tents, the rest in the fields. Morning and evening hard bread was given out by the Black Monks.

Mordec and Gus stood out among the crowd because of their height and the colour of their hair, and were noticed particularly by some ten or twelve beggar children who called them Angels and came every evening to dance about them in the fields, singing songs of praise. This drew the attention of some Black Monks who watched the nightly caper from a distance. 'Don't look at them,' Mordec advised the children, 'and maybe they'll keep away.'

Twice in the night they woke to find persons furtively searching their bags, but both times they were only holy penitents looking for something to steal and were easily driven off with growls and lifted daggers.

On the third day Lily hired an old horse from a foppish priest who was leading it as a spare. She let Charlotte ride behind her. This made the dancer very happy. She blew her trumpet now and then, but not too often because Lily said it 'hammered her ears'.

When the Great Progress reached Nebulo, Lily wanted to plunge into the city at once in search of her mother. 'I know she's here, I feel it,' she said.

But Gus and Mordec wouldn't start on a hazardous mission which might draw attention to themselves while the town was full of militant Christians. They waited in a meadow near the city gates. Lily was too excited to sleep, but the others dozed from time to time. Gus was roused from a dream by a new and troubling thought. 'What will your mother feel about Vikings coming to rescue her?' he asked Lily.

'I'll explain,' she said abruptly.

Mordec too had been thinking about Queen Gloria. 'Is your mother like a Valkyrie?' he asked. 'Valkyries say if a warrior is worthy of going to Valhalla.'

'She's not like any woman of the Vikings,' Lily said with high disdain.

'Like an Amazon then? I read about the Amazons in one of my mother's books. They were braver and stronger than men and could ride horses faster and shoot arrows truer than the archers of the Greeks. They were ruled by a queen, and some say they cut off one of their breasts so they could use their bows more easily.'

'That would be very sore. My mother never did anything like that. But she *will* lead an army to victory against you. One of our queens defeated the Romans about a thousand years ago and she's like her.'

If Gloria really was the kind of leader who arose once in a thousand years, Mordec thought, Ingolf and Rorick had had good reason to capture her and take her far from England. But it was too late to think about that. He had no choice now but to honour his word, so lightly given, to try and set her free.

Their wait was long. Whatever it was that was going on in the city—more protests by the Official Poor perhaps—the doing of good in there was taking longer than usual. The elephant didn't lead the procession out again until late in the night, and it was morning before the last of the holy penitents emerged and started along the road. Then Mordec, Gus, Lily and Charlotte took off their crosses and entered Nebulo.

the exile's lament

They lingered uncertainly on a concourse which was already crowded although it was still quite early in the morning, and were wondering how to set about finding the house of Ingolf when they were greeted in a trembling voice by a lanky old man.

'You are from the Northlands, aren't you?' he asked.

The boys nodded.

'Vikings?'

They nodded again.

'I haven't seen my homeland for many a long year,' he sighed, 'and I miss it painfully.'

His eyes watered, from grief or age or both.

'Why don't you go back if you miss it?'

The old man seemed not to hear Gus's question. He asked them their names and gave his own as Leif son of Halga.

'I am a poet,' he said. 'But as I compose poetry only in my own language which few here understand, I shall never enjoy the glory that's my due.'

'Do you know all the Vikings who live in Nebulo?' Lily asked.

'Yes, yes. We are a small group, and dying off. It's good to see young visitors from the homeland. Are you thinking of settling here?'

'No, we—'

'Would you care to listen to a poem of mine? Come this way, where it's quieter. Here's a fallen column, almost overgrown with bleeding-heart and blue-wanderer. A good place for me to recite my lament.'

When they were all seated in a row on the column, he stood facing them and announced, *The Lament of Leif the Exile.*'

He crossed his arms on his chest, gripped his shoulders with gnarled hands, frowned, shut his eyes, tipped his head back and began:

Listen to me! I am Leif son of Halga.
Hear how I mourn for my lost land,
An exile forever, ever a wanderer
Lost to his kin as if dead, but still living,
Alone on the waves of time's wild sea.
Once I served Eyiolf the king who was hairless,
Whose head was as smooth as a sea-worn boulder,
Whose arm was as strong as the arm of Thor almost

'You really liked Eyiolf the Bald?' Mordec interrupted. 'Come on! Nobody did. He squeezed out taxes until nobody had anything left. He murdered thousands in all sorts of horrible ways. Everyone dreaded him. Sometimes he had people tortured just for his own entertainment. He was one of the cruelest rulers who ever lived.'

'Yes, he was cruel,' Leif conceded, dropping his arms and gazing gloomily into the distance. 'I know that. Who should know it better than I? I was one of his Assistant Executioners. I didn't exactly enjoy the job, but it was safer than most. I'm not saying he wasn't cruel. But he was fair. Cruel but fair.'

'Fair? Eyiolf? How can you say he was fair?'

'I can say it because—because he was equally cruel to everybody. Almost.'

Mordec laughed.

Leif turned to him. 'Listen—it doesn't matter any more what Eyiolf was, or what you think of him. The point is, what do you think of the poem? The poem is all. Art may scorn reality. Art is free to soar above mere facts. Now tell me frankly. Do you or don't you like the poem?'

Mordec thought it was a dull and stupid poem but he didn't want to hurt Leif's feelings by saying so, especially as the fellow was such an old misery-guts already.

'It's fine, fine,' he said. 'Now could you—'

'You haven't heard it all.'

'Another time perhaps. We're in a hurry now.'

'We're on an urgent mission,' Lily said. 'We've got to find someone.'

'Do you know—you must know—where Eyiolf's son Ingolf lives?' Gus said.

'Yes, I do. He has poetry-evenings sometimes at his house and I've taken part a few times. He's a good payer. My fees for reciting at Ingolf's poetry-evenings have more than once fished me out of deep water.'

'And do you know where Captain Rorick lives?' Lily asked.

'Rorick? Of course. He's captain of Ingolf's guard.'

'He lives in Ingolf's house?'

'Yes. But he doesn't attend the poetry evenings. He's not exactly a man of high culture or refined tastes, your Captain Rorick. But the lady is.'

'The lady,' Lily repeated.

'"La Belladonna", everyone calls her. 'Though she's not Italian.'

'Ingolf s wife?' Mordec asked.

'Ingolf's wife? Surely not. I never heard that he had one.'

'Who's this lady then?'

'La Belladonna is Captain Rorick's wife.'

'And you say she's not Italian?'

'No. And she's not a Viking. I'm not sure what she is.'

'Oh never mind all that!' Lily said impatiently. 'We don't need him to describe the whole household. Let's just get him to show us the house.'

Leif agreed to lead them there. It wasn't far, he said, and he went on chatting as they pushed their way through the hot crowded streets. 'Very central, in fact. A grand place. Quite the palazza.' He sounded slightly envious. 'Ingolf managed to get a good load of his father's treasure safely away before the invaders came, you see.'

Mordec, walking beside him, asked, 'Do you know if they have a woman captive there? An Englishwoman?'

'Now you mention it, I think I heard that La Belladonna is an Englishwoman.'

'No I don't mean Rorick's wife. I mean a lady kept against her will. Kept in chains, perhaps.'

'In chains? A lady? They might go in for that, I suppose. Nebulo's full of strange goings on. Decadent place this. There now—that's the house you want. I'll leave you. I only go in when I'm invited. I hope I'll see you there when next I come to recite.'

the iron garden

Lily's excitement mounted as they approached Ingolf's house. It was big and solid, built of reddish stone. There were bars over the windows.

'More like a fortress than a palace,' Mordec said.

Gus stepped back and looked the place over. 'It's not going to be easy to get in,' he said.

'Why don't we just knock on the door and ask to see Ingolf?' Lily said through closed teeth.

'You think they'll *ask* us in?'

'Why not?'

In each of the pair of iron-studded doors was a small cross-barred window and beneath each of them a bronze kitten whose tail was hinged to make a knocker. Mordec lifted both the tails.

'Wait,' Gus said. 'You realize we're walking right into the enemy's stronghold? It's just possible that we won't come out alive.'

'What should we do then?' Mordec asked.

'Knock,' Lily said.

'It could be one of the last things you ever do,' Gus said. 'Let me do it.'

'Go on, Mordec, hurry up and knock,' Lily said.

'And brace yourself for battle,' Gus said.

Mordec banged on the doors with the kittens. A part of a face peered out through one of the small windows. Then a bent old man opened the door.

'Yes?' he said in a cracked, frail voice.

Mordec gave his name and asked if he and his companions could please see Ingolf son of Eyiolf.

'Who are you?'

They hadn't prepared an answer to this question.

'Travellers from the North,' Mordec said.

'Wait.' The old man shut the door and re-opened it a minute later.

'Step in. Leave your bags here and hand over your swords,' the old man said.

'Our swords?' Gus repeated, hardly believing his ears.

'You can keep your daggers,' the old man said, 'but hand over your swords or you don't go a step further.'

Gus still hesitated, trying to catch Mordec's eye. If they were going to fight their way through they must make their strike now or never. But just at that moment a number of young men—how many it was hard to tell—appeared behind the old man, all wearing swords.

Mordec said, 'Let's do what he says. Just this once.'

'We may have no other chance,' Gus said. But the other two had already given their swords to the old man. Gus reluctantly leant his against the wall.

'Right. This way then.' The armed men stood aside and the visitors followed the old man through two large empty rooms and into a third, even larger. The man who rose to greet them was not tall but not short, not old but not young, and he was wearing nothing but a loin-cloth and many gold ornaments. His hair was gilded and arranged like leaves. His eyelids were painted gold, and so were the nails on his fingers and toes. In one hand he held a white handkerchief and used it frequently to dab at his nose and eyes. Behind him stood a young man, armed.

'What do you want?' the almost-naked man asked. 'Say what you hab to say and be quick about it please.' He spoke softly but nervously and touched the cloth to his nostrils.

'You are Ingolf son of Eyiolf?' Gus said.

'Yes that's who I ab.'

Gus put an arm about Lily's shoulders and together they stepped forward.

Lily said, 'I am Lily daughter of—'

'You are a febale? Odds-bods! D'you hear that, Barcello? This is dot a boy. All the sabe, I'b charbed to beet you,' Ingolf said politely. 'To what do I owe the pleasure of your visit?'

'I want to know what you've done with my mother, Gloria Queen of the Fenreach.'

Ingolf opened his mouth, shut it again, and keeping his eyes fixed on Lily took a step or two backwards and sat down slowly on a bronze bench. He turned to the young man.

'I do think, Barcello, it would be best if we got Rory id here.'

Barcello went out through an open door into a courtyard.

'Do you know where she is?' Lily asked.

'Your buther? And she's—Queen Gloria did you say? Well yes, I do, actually.'

'Where?'

'Er. Er. Ah, Rory.' Ingolf sounded much relieved.

A big man, a Viking, but clean-shaven like an Italian and dressed like an Italian, came in from the courtyard.

'Ah, here you are,' he called heartily as he entered. 'All the way from the Far North, I hear. And in your case, Queen Lily, er—' he looked first at Charlotte, who slightly shook her head, then at each of the others in turn, finally fixing his gaze on Lily—'all the way from England, I understand. How do I know? Simple. I've been sitting out there listening.'

'Are you Captain Rorick?' Gus asked.

'Rory. Call me Rory. Everybody does. Here in Italy we are not formal. Won't you sit down? No? Mind if I do?' He sat on another bronze bench and placed his thumbs on his knees. 'Now what can I do for you?'

'Do you know where my mother is?' Lily tried again, this time through her teeth, keeping her patience with some difficulty. 'Queen Gloria. The lady you seized in her own queendom and carried off to Eyiolf's fortress. I've come on a long quest for her, to fetch her home. Tell me please—is she in this house?'

'She is. Your quest is at an end.'

'Not yet. Will you take me to her please?'

'I will. I'll take you to her myself.' He rose. 'Come with me please.'

'You bust excuse be,' Ingolf said, 'for not cubbing too. It's the flowers, you see. They utterly destroy be.'

It was hard to know what he meant. There were no flowers to be seen. Not even in the courtyard across which they followed Rory. It was a garden in which nothing grew. There was a pond with a fountain, and paving stones, and iron pots with iron trees. Metal 'creepers' with gilded leaves spiraled up the columns.

Rory was chatting to them affably, but Lily took in nothing he was saying. She stared fiercely at his back, and more than once her right hand moved towards the dagger in her belt, but dropped again. The men guarding her mother must be near, she thought, and this was not the moment to risk starting a battle.

'It's his nose, you see,' Rory was saying. 'No sooner do the buds of May appear than he comes down with hay-fever, and it lasts until the first cold snap of winter. Poor boy. Imagine what it must be like to be the victim of flowers. His Moorish physician told him the only remedy was to keep away from them. He can do that here at home, more or less. But when he goes out, there they are, lying in wait to ambush him at every turn. Feathers too have turned against him. He used to adore feathers. Now he shuns them. Of course they're easier to avoid than flowers. Never, never *dare* he step into *her* quarters—as you will understand when you see …'

the captive queen

The captain opened a last pair of doors and led the way into a high vaulted room full of flowering plants. It was also full of couches, cushions, little gilded tables strewn with ornaments, and birds in cages. The light was soft and rosy as though filtered through pink petals.

'Darling,' Rory said, 'a huge surprise for you. Guess who's come all the way from England to find you.' He turned to Lily. 'I'll leave you to your happy reunion.'

Gus and Mordec stared after him with wondering looks as he hurried out and shut the door.

A woman's voice said 'Boys? Who are you?'

She was a pretty woman, her rather full body lightly draped in gauze, her golden curls elaborately arranged. She wore a jewel on her forehead, a fine gold chain about her neck, another round an ankle, and golden sandals. She stood at the far end of the room looking at them uncertainly.

Lily was looking uncertain too. 'Mother?' she said, and pulled off her cap.

'Lily? No! It can't be! Darling, is it you?' Gloria hurried across the room, smiling, lifting up her arms, but Lily drew back.

'Are you my mother?' she asked.

'Yes darling. If you are Lily. Don't you recognize me?'

Lily gazed at the soft pink smiling face, let her eyes wander over it, and said at last. 'It *is* you. It really is.' She let herself be embraced then, but Mordec saw her shut her eyes tightly. Gus smiled as he watched. He was startled by a tap on his shoulder.

'Come,' Mordec said, 'let's leave them.'

Gus opened his mouth to protest, but on second thoughts turned and followed Mordec from the room. When he'd shut the door Mordec grinned broadly.

'What?' Gus said.

'I don't think we've got much to worry about, do you?'

'You can't judge by what she looks like. Lily can look all prettied-up too, but—'

'You think that pretty lady could lead an army?'

Gus looked down. 'I think Lily will be disappointed.'

'I think so to,' Mordec said, and laughed.

They returned to the room they'd started from and there was Charlotte sitting beside Ingolf, chatting brightly. She stopped when they came in and called out, 'I told him I was a dancer and he wants me to dance here tonight.'

'Is she a good dancer?' Ingolf asked.

Mordec said 'Yes.'

'Glad to hear it. Now cub along, let's drink chilled wide. In the courtyard. Cad I send away by guard? You don't bean to burder be do you?'

'I don't think so. Not now,' Mordec said. 'We might've if you'd tried to keep Lily from her mother.'

'Not a very girlish sort of girl,' Ingolf commented, spreading himself on an iron bench beside the pond and dabbing at the red rims of his nostrils.

'What d'you mean?' Gus asked, frowning.

'Duthing, dear boy. Duthing at all. In all truth, her girlishness or lack of it is of doe interest to be whatsoever. Here cubs the wide. And these delectable little sweetbeats are bade of frangipade, of which you have doe doubt dever heard. Taste and be easy.'

'It's not drugged is it, the wine?' Gus asked.

'Dear be, you are suspicious! Watch—I pour, I drink—there. Dow you cad feel safe doing the sabe.'

They poured, each for himself, and drank. The wine was wonderfully cold and went down easily. The fountain made a gentle splashing sound. Instead of the armed struggle they had more than half expected they were simply enjoying themselves.

Charlotte slipped away in search of Lily and found her. She was sitting close to Gloria on a couch and Gloria was stroking her face with soft pink fingers. Neither of them took any notice of Charlotte as she came quietly into the room. She crept among the flowering plants and saw that Gloria was shedding a few tears and Lily was wiping them away from her mother's cheeks with the back of her sunburnt hand.

'You must be happy now, Mother. It's all over, your ordeal. I know it must have been terrible. I've come to take you home.'

'My darling, it's wonderful to see you, it really is. My little girl. How you've grown!'

'I have a horse waiting for you in England, Mother, such as you could never have known before. The swiftest in the world. Maelstrom I call him. He's not at Goosegarth now, but I'll soon fetch him home. Mother! England will celebrate when the news spreads that you are back. The kings and earls will flock to your side. We'll build a great army, and even if half of it falls, we'll drive away the Vikings and maybe you will become queen of all England.'

'Celebrate, yes,' Gloria said, picking up the only word of Lily's which stirred pleasure in her. 'We must celebrate your coming. We'll have a grand celebration tonight. Ingolf will arrange it. He loves doing that sort of thing. He's good at it too.'

'You won't have to live like this any more.' Lily waved her arm as if to do away with everything in the room.

'We must get you something lovely to wear,' her mother said. 'We must get you lots of lovely things.'

'And me?' The question made them look about to see where it came from.

'I need something lovely to wear too.'

'Charlotte?' Lily called, 'Where are you?'

'Here.'

And there she was, looking at them through a cascade of lilac.

'I told the man that I'd dance for him tonight. I'll make up a new dance. So you see there're things I need. You must get them for me, Mother.'

'You mustn't call her Mother. She's Queen Gloria to you.'

'But I don't have a mother,' Charlotte said, suddenly bursting into noisy crying.

Gloria went and drew her out of the lilac bushes and brought her to the couch. 'Sit here, on the other side of me, so I can put my arms round both of you, and you may call me Mother. And of course you shall also have something pretty to wear.' Charlotte stopped crying as suddenly as she'd started. 'Tell me, Lily, who is this enchanting little girl?'

'Charlotte. She's just my maidservant.'

'I'm glad you have one, darling.'

'I didn't want one. I didn't ask her. And I didn't buy her. *She* asked *me*. I must admit she's been quite useful. When someone drugged me and tied me up and tried to take me back to England, I don't know why, Charlotte—.'

'You'll tell me all about it later, darling. I'm dying to hear. But now I must have my spiced wine and a spoonful of oats in honey—it's all I'm allowed because I'm a little overweight—and you two will join me, I hope, and then I'll take you to the silk-merchant and the gem-dealer.' Gloria reached for a silver bell on the small gilded table beside her and shook it into merry life.

'At least they don't treat you badly, Mother,' Lily said. Gloria didn't seem to hear.

Later, as they drove through busy streets, Lily tried again. 'Do they let you go out in a wagon like this whenever you like?'

'Chariot, darling. My own chariot. And my own horses to pull it. And my own Egyptian to drive it. Doesn't he look handsome all brown and gold? I'm proud of him, you know, but I sometimes wonder if Rorick got him for me so he'd have someone to tell him where I go.'

'But you can go where you like, when you like? As long as you don't escape?'

'Of course I go where I like. But what d'you mean by "escape"?'

'They never try to stop you?'

'Who d'you mean, darling?'

'Ingolf and Rorick.'

'Ingolf? Ingolf doesn't mind what I do. Rory gets a bit jealous sometimes, but I always tell him he has nothing to be jealous about. To me he's still the most attractive man I've ever met.'

'Are you saying that—Mother, are you telling me—I mean, you didn't go away with him because you *wanted* to, did you?'

'Well, I—'

'So he didn't force you to go with him. Did he?'

'Oh look, my dears, over there! Puppets. Look, Charlotte.'

'Stop!' Charlotte shouted, 'I want to see them.'

And not only to see them. Charlotte insisted on going behind the scenes to watch how the puppets were worked. She wanted to learn how to *do* it, she said. But Gloria said they must hurry on if they were to get everything they needed by nightfall.

'You must give me money, Mother,' Charlotte demanded, 'and let me buy what I want.'

Gloria laughed and put a purse in the small hand.

'Will you find your way home?' Gloria called. Too late. Charlotte had vanished in the crowd.

'You call it home, Mother?' Lily said. 'Ingolf's house?'

'It's my house too. And, well, it's sort of home from home, isn't it darling? Now will Charlotte get lost do you think?'

'Never,' Lily assured her.

'Ah, Signora Belladonna!' the merchants greeted Gloria, and Gloria smiled and asked to see the best they had.

'Mother, are you married to Rorick?'

'Oh you must keep that one on,' Gloria said, meaning the garment which had just been cut and stitched and sashed more or less on her body. Lily let herself be dressed, smiling at her mother's pleasure. But she resolved that if ever she married Gus she would have only boy children.

When Gloria told the friends she met that this was her daughter, some of them *said* they were surprised to hear that Gloria had a daughter 'so grown up', but to Lily they didn't look surprised at all.

'I *could* say you're my niece,' Gloria said as they drove home, 'but in time they'd know the truth, so I simply say you were born when I was very, very young.'

'What d'you mean, "they'd know in time"? We're not staying long.'

'Oh please don't talk about going just yet. To-morrow if you like, but not now.'

'Don't you want to go home to the Fenreach as soon as you can?'

'Hush, darling! Tonight we celebrate. Tomorrow if you wish we'll talk about life and destiny and travel and—'

'And who will fight for the freedom of our land?'

'Yes and that too.'

puppets

In the evening a large company, in gauze and gold and gems, assembled at the house of Ingolf. They dined and drank and laughed, until Ingolf tinkled a bell and asked for silence 'for Charlotte, a dancer dewly arrived in this city'.

Curtains opened to reveal a small section of the marble floor lit by a row of small lamps which threw their light along the marble but were shielded from the eyes of the watchers. Someone invisible started playing a tune on a pipe. A little puppet, about the length of two hands, dressed as a lady of Nebulo, hopped and skipped jerkily across the floor. Another, rather bigger, dressed the same, emerged where it had disappeared and danced back the other way. Then another and another came out, from this side or that, each bigger than the last. The movements were the same for all of them as the strings were pulled this way or that to raise a leg by the knee, lift or drop the arms, turn the head, or let the whole doll flop from the hips.

Strange, Mordec thought, that Charlotte had decided not to dance to-night and have a go instead at something new and different. She was doing it well enough for a beginner, he supposed, but what

would Ingolf's guests think of it? And as if in answer
to his unspoken question, a young man remarked to
Ingolf softly but clearly that it wasn't bad but he'd
seen better and wasn't it a bit repetitive? Ingolf raised
a finger and whispered, 'Wait!'

The last doll was as big as a child, about as big
as Charlotte herself, Lily thought. It hopped and
skipped exactly as the smallest one had, just as stiff-
ly and jerkily. The wooden face was the same, only
bigger, with the same pointed nose and circles of red
on the cheeks. You could see the nailheads, black
dots on the pale wood, where the hands were jointed
into the arms. It finished by flopping from the hips
in imitation of a bow. Its arms dangled and it swung
slightly from side to side, hanging on its invisible
strings. Then it straightened up, pulled a mask from
its face, bowed like a living child, and as a living child
ran off. For a moment the audience was silent with
astonishment, then burst into tremendous applause.
Guests went up to Ingolf and praised the perfor-
mance as though he'd given it himself, and Ingolf
looked delighted and said 'Thank you, thank you.'

a confession

Lily allowed Gloria to try pieces of jewelry on her in front of a glass mirror, but her thoughts were fixed on other things.

'When will we start for home, Mother? Will Rorick give us an armed escort to Genova? Do ships often sail from there to England?'

At last Gloria sighed, sat on a couch and patted the cushion. 'Come and sit beside me, darling, I have something important to say to you. It's—it's a sort of confession, darling.'

'A confession? You mean about Rorick not forcing you to go with him? I've understood that. And it's alright. I forgive you. I don't understand how you could go with him and leave me, and leave the Fenreach, but I forgive you. I suppose it isn't really such a big surprise to me that you wanted to go with Rorick. Grandmother always said that's what happened.'

'Did she? Bertha did? I hope she understood why. She had a lot to do with it.'

'What d'you mean?'

'I had to get away from *her*, darling.'

'From Bertha? But she wasn't a bad mother, was she? She's always been good to me.'

'No no, you miss the point. She was a very good mother. But no man would look at me while Bertha was there too. At first I even thought that Rory was in love with her, so I told him how she'd fed Osvald son of Olvir to the little lioness, and then I got him to promise to take me away with him.'

'I see,' Lily said slowly. 'I see,' and sat in silence, letting her mother wind a lock of her hair round a soft pink finger.

At last she said, 'You don't want to come back with me, do you?'

Gloria shook her head. 'You'll have to forgive me again. You've come all this way and risked such dangers to get to me and now it must seem that it was all for nothing. But don't look at it that way, darling. We're together again. You can stay here with me. It's a much better life, darling, you must see that. You must see—I couldn't go back to that—that run-down farm and those stupid cackling geese, and the cold wet weather all the year round, and the—the sheer boredom of life in the Fenreach, darling, I couldn't! You see? You see?'

Lily turned her head away, for once in her life close to tears, for the loss of a hope. But she braced herself and turned back to tell Gloria that she couldn't see anything of the sort.

Then Gloria cried. Lily looked at the bent head with its carefully arranged curls, at the silk-clad shoulders of this soft, sweet-natured, if also self-indulgent woman shaken with sobs, and she felt not only compassion and kindness rising in her, but a sudden wisdom beyond her years. She embraced her, wiped away her tears and told her that she understood, that she really didn't mind, not one bit, except that she would always miss her dreadfully.

'I can see you're happy here, Mother. But are you sure it'll always be like this? What if Rorick dies? What will happen when you grow old and have no family of your own to look after you?'

'Please don't say things like that,' Gloria begged.

They rocked awhile in each other's arms, and then Gloria, feeling calmer and even quite contented again, sat up straight and said, 'You know, Lily darling, you're far better able to lead an army into war and make treaties with the little kings and the great earls than I am. Anyone only has to look at the two of us to know that! You're the one who'll ride that swift horse into battle. And you'll win. Rory says you're the only person he's ever even heard of that he'd be afraid to meet on the battlefield.'

'Rorick said that?' Lily stared at her for a moment and then burst out laughing, and Gloria laughed too, though the tears were still shining in her eyes. 'What has he heard about me?'

'I—I told him about a battle against the Cymric Celts which you led when you were only twelve. When you won a famous victory and personally slayed most of them.'

'He believed you?'

Gloria nodded. 'I told the story so well I believed it too. *Didn't* something of the sort actually happen?'

'No.'

'No?'

'Well, perhaps it did.'

They laughed. The lost Queen of the Fenreach had not lost her wits. She kept them safe and took them out when she needed them. 'But what you said about the future,' Gloria said, miserable again, 'I can't help thinking that you may be right, and I'm afraid.'

'I was only saying it to get you to come home with me. I don't know if it will be like that. Why should it be?'

'It won't be?' The mother appealed to the daughter as if the mother were the child. 'Say it won't be.'

'It won't be.'

'But now you're only saying that to comfort me, aren't you? How do you know?'

'I don't know, but Sam of the West knows, and he told me what the future will be like. He is a great magician and I believe him.'

'Tell me then, what will it be like? What does the great magician say?'

'Let me try and remember.' She would say nothing of Sam's dire predictions for the first few centuries of the new millennium—the Church spreading its power and 'reaching into every land and every home to enforce its will with iron and fire'. She recalled things her mother would like to hear. 'He says that one day there will be carriages that need no beasts to draw them. You'll have one of your own, of course, and when you want to go anywhere you'll just step into it and order it to take you there and off it will go.'

'No waiting for horses to be put between the shafts? No horse-mess in the streets? No Egyptian driver who could tell Rory where I've been? I'll like that.' She was quiet for a few moments as she thought about her magic carriage. Then, 'Tell me more,' she said. 'What else did he say?'

'He said that the time will come when you'll never need to carry coins. You'll write down a sum of money on a piece of paper and give it to the merchant and he'll take it to the Lombards and they'll give him the coins. Everyone will do that so there'll be no more robbers on the roads.'

'I shall like buying things with bits of paper. I won't have to explain to Rory where all the money's gone. Tell me more.'

'What else? Let me think. Ah, yes. There'll be a thing you can speak into that will carry your words to someone far away. Or near, but in another room. If you wake in the morning and you want Ingolf to arrange a party for you, you won't need to rise and put on gowns and have your hair dressed just to go and speak to him. You'll stay in bed and speak through this thing. Then he'll use one like it to order food and wine and invite your friends.'

'Could I speak to you from here when you're back in England?'

'Yes. Though I think it will take longer for such things to come to England than to Nebulo.'

'Perhaps with self-driving carriages and no robbers on the road we'll be able to visit each other often?'

'Perhaps.'

Gloria sighed, consoled and happy again.

Lily didn't tell Gloria that Sam had also said it would take another thousand years for such things as self-driving carriages and far-speakers to be invented. Let her look forward to an ever rosier future of more ease, more dresses, more jewels, more feasts and entertainments, more chatter, more fun. Lily would say no more of England's plight or a queen's duty. But she would go home soon and start preparing for war as best she could, knowing at least that the lost Queen of the Fenreach could not have done it better.

the enemy cornered

The night was hot. Lily lay down in her dress of gauze on the wet paving stones beside the pond and stirred her hands in the water, breaking up the reflection of the full moon. 'Mother won't be coming back with me to England,' she told Gus and Mordec.

'I thought she wouldn't,' Mordec said. 'Anyone can see she likes it here.'

'She came away with Rorick because she wanted to. She wanted to be with him more than she wanted to be with me. And now she'd much rather be a lady here than a queen in England.'

'The crazy thing is,' Gus said, 'I'd be the best person in the world to ride beside you into battle, and there's nothing I'd like to do more—than lead an army into battle I mean,' he explained quickly, glancing round at Mordec. 'And I can't do it, because you've chosen me to be the enemy. Us, I mean.'

'I didn't *choose* you to be the enemy, Gus. You *are* the enemy.'

'Yet I came willingly to help you find your mother, knowing your reason for wanting her back.'

'But only because you didn't believe that she would make any difference to your grip on swaths of England.'

'I didn't know that for sure. And anyway I told you—if ever your English army marches against us, I'll have no choice but to fight you. I told you that I'd seek you out and force you into single combat and one of us at least would have to die, but it would be a story of heroes and the skalds would tell it for hundreds of years to come.'

'So you never believed me when I said that my mother could unite the rulers of England? How could you know before you came here that I was right or wrong when I said she would be our warrior-queen?'

'I didn't know.'

'She might have been exactly what I said, yet you came to help me find her. Why?'

'I thought maybe you just felt sad at losing her. And I didn't think she'd change anything much even though I thought of her as a warrior-queen, because you're a warrior-queen anyway.'

Lily laughed, remembering what her mother had said to Rorick about her defeat of a Cymric army when she was only twelve years old. She told them the story. 'Do you believe it? One of Eyiolf's captains afraid to meet *me* on the battlefield!'

Mordec joined in her laughter, the two of them looking at each other and sharing a joke that Gus couldn't see. He demanded sharply, 'But what's funny about that?'

Mordec shook his head and wandered off. Gus watched him go and thought, 'We could do without Mordec.'

'Gus, why don't you laugh like Mordec?' Lily asked.

'Like Mordec?' Gus said. 'Who'd want to be like Mordec? He's not a true Viking.'

'All the better.'

'He's looking for a fight and one of these days he'll get it.'

'And will the skalds tell the story for hundreds of years to come?'

'Are you mocking me? You are. But why?'

'I can't explain. There are some things that can't be explained.'

'Like jokes?'

'Yes. Like jokes.'

Mordec found Rorick pacing among the columns and sipping from a silver cup.

'Ah, Mordec,' he said genially, 'it's you. I hear you'll be leaving us soon. Gloria will be really sorry. We all will be.'

'Sure.'

'I hear the little Charlotte will not be going with you. Did you know that? Ingolf asked her to stay.' He laughed and drank. 'Amazing child. Does what she wants, when she wants, how she wants. And what a dancer she is. Though I believe she's older than she looks.' He sipped his drink and Mordec let silence settle between them for a minute or two.

Then he said quietly, 'It was you, wasn't it, who tried to stop us getting here?'

'What d'you mean? I didn't even know you were coming. We were all more surprised than we've ever been in our lives—'

'Is that so? Lily might believe you, and if Lily does Gus will. But I don't.'

Mordec spoke quietly. He was aware that what he was saying might provoke the man, but he wanted Rorick to answer certain questions.

'Lily was pleased by something you said about her,' he went on.

'What was that?'

'That you'd be afraid to meet her on the battle-field.' Rorick laughed his loud, hearty laugh. 'Yes, I did say it. And that was before I met her. Another amazing girl, Lily.'

'The sort of girl who would carry someone off if she wanted to, whatever the dangers. You couldn't risk that, could you?'

There was a longer silence now. Mordec kept his eyes on the captain's face and the captain looked anywhere but at Mordec. He drank, strolled, gazed up at the moon.

Mordec said quietly but insistently, 'It *was* you, wasn't it? I want to know.'

'Me? What are you talking about?'

'*You did know* we were coming, didn't you? You must've known. Though I'm not sure how. Did Julius send you a message? Perhaps it was tied to the foot of a dove, or perhaps it was stowed in a trader's bag—but somehow you heard. I also don't know how you arranged for a bribe to be paid as far away as the domain of Sec-et-Doux. But you did, didn't you?'

Rorick drank and said nothing.

'Tell me how you knew we were coming. How you knew the route we'd take. Who your messenger was to Sec-et-Doux.'

Rorick leant his back against a column, gold leaves shining above him in the moonlight. He sighed. 'All right,' he said. 'You've guessed so much you may as well know it all. I'll tell you. If you'll keep it to yourself. If you give me your word you won't tell Lily.'

'I'll keep it to myself until we're well away from here, if that's what's worrying you. You don't want Lily leaping on you with a sword.'

Rorick said, 'You're funny, Mordec. But a bit too clever for my taste.'

'You won't have to put up with me for much longer. But I want to know how you did it.'

'It wasn't Julius who let me know. It was Roxane. Her father was one of us.'

'And how did she do it?'

'You guessed. Foot of a dove. A dove named Po-Valley Central. We have her here, in Gloria's room, awaiting a carrier to take her back.'

'Go on. You may as well tell me the rest.'

'My messenger at Sec-et-Doux? Guess.'

'The priest?'

'Priest? No no. You've seen no priests in our company, have you? We have nothing to do with priests if we can help it.'

'Was it Timble the leader of the dancers?'

Rorick shook his head.

'Who then?'

'Do you remember a strong man performing at
the Castle?'

Mordec did. He looked up at the moon and the
name came back to him. 'Igor—Igor the Rus?'

'He too was one of us. Very young in those days,
but already a human elephant. He's one of my spies.
I give them gold from time to time. They bring me
news, they carry out certain errands for me. Igor's
not the cleverest. Ingolf has him here to entertain
us—or, rather, to entertain me, he says, seeing that
I don't care for poetry-recitals and things like that.
And I get Igor to do small favors for me. But I have
to be very exact in my instructions. I left a bit too
much to him this time. Bribing the dancers to dress
up as animals to try scaring you so much that you'd
turn round and go home was his own idea and not
a good one.'

'But how did you get your orders to him? How
did you know we'd go to the Castle?'

'I didn't. Not for sure. But there aren't many routes
you could take to get here. I'd sent messages along
the trade-routes before you'd even set out from Julius.
I had men waiting for you in every likely place.'

'Go on. What about the Cids? Do you give them
gold? Was it on your orders that they drugged us
and robbed us?'

'They do what I tell them. I don't pay them. They
do it out of pure clean fear.'

'Brinjolf said he didn't know where you were.'

'Of course he did. You had to be deceived. They
do what I tell them, the Cids. Not that there's much

they *can* do for me any more. If it wasn't for the Sichi they'd forget they were ever warriors. Spend their time dressing up as women and acting out love stories. Their sons and grandsons are more useful. Most of them are here in Nebulo. Nine in this very house. I see to it that they don't forget who they are. A small army under my command as long as I live.'

'What do you use it for?'

'Protection.'

Mordec grew thoughtful.

Rorick said, 'I understand the Cids used *your* money to bribe the princess from Baghdad?' He chuckled, a slightly drunken sound. 'Sorry to laugh, but it *is* quite funny.'

'Would Gloria think it funny if she knew?'

It was plain enough even in the pale light of the moon that this question disturbed the captain. The face he turned to Mordec was wary.

'Knew what?'

'That you tried to stop Lily coming here. After those silly warning beasts failed you knew she could only be stopped by force. She'd have to be drugged and bound and taken away from us when we weren't looking. I guess you told the Cids that Lily mustn't be harmed but it would be all right to kill *us*?'

'Only if really necessary. I didn't want Lily coming back to these parts to avenge you. Besides, I was feeling merciful.'

'But you were taking quite a risk, weren't you? I mean, traders and slavers will take a bribe from anyone to do this or that but once they've been paid they can go and do whatever they want—make a slave of her, or kill her. I can't see Lily letting herself be kept as a slave. She'd rather be killed, I think. It was just lucky for her that the Princess Starling was passing that way at that time.'

'It wasn't just lucky. She'd been here awhile in Nebulo. A sentimental lady. When I heard from the Cids that they'd got you I told them to watch out for her and make the arrangements. I knew she'd treat Lily well, as Gloria's daughter.'

'I'd say that just being made a prisoner is being treated badly. I've been a prisoner so I know. Anyway, you've told me how you did it. It was quite cunning really,'

'I've had to be cunning to survive.'

'Surviving doesn't make you feel ashamed?'

'Not any more. I suffered from shame at first, quite a bit, but Eyiolf's treasure consoled me.'

'And having Queen Gloria for a wife?'

'She's a great comfort too.'

'She trusts you, doesn't she?'

Rorick narrowed his eyes. 'What are you getting at?'

'Lily—'

'Lily's alright. I haven't hurt her.'

'You tried to.'

'I tried to thwart her attempt to come and fetch Gloria away, yes. But I didn't succeed, did I?'

'You had her drugged, tied up—'

'But you said you wouldn't tell her.'

'I won't tell her. I was only thinking of telling her mother.'

'Ah! Well, I don't think you should.'

This time it was Mordec who kept silent. Rorick kept his eyes on him as he lifted his cup to his lips. Finding it empty he shouted for it to be refilled. 'And a cup for my honoured friend,' he ordered. 'Let's drink to our friendship, Mordec, and to honour between us as Viking warriors.'

Mordec took the cup and looked down at the wine which seemed black in the moonlight.

'I need something from you,' he said.

'What? Of course. Anything I can do, I'd be glad. Name it.'

'For one thing I want our things back from the Cids. Our bags and weapons. And my gold.'

'You'll get it. Give me seven days and you'll have it all back. Though maybe there's not much left of the gold. Maybe the Princess Starling got all of it.'

'It doesn't have to be the same coins. Just the same amount.'

'I'll try. I promise. I'll do my best. Will that satisfy you? If you get your things back you won't take tales to Gloria?'

'There's one other thing.'

'What?'

'Let me tell you about the town where my grandfather lives. You see, it's in danger and maybe you could help.'

queen gloria forgives

'So, darling,' Rorick said to Gloria, 'I promised him I'd send a hundred men to help guard this town his grandfather lives in.'

'And you're sure, Rory,' Gloria said, 'that he doesn't suspect me? Because I don't want Lily ever to know that I asked you to try and stop her coming. I remember that you didn't want to do it. In fact it took me hours to persuade you.'

'I know. But I did try. I'm only sorry I failed. Forgive me, darling.'

'I forgive you because *I'm* not sorry at all really. I'm glad she came. She's a marvelous child in her own way, and I'm sure she'll be a great ruler of the poor old Fenreach. I feel now it was wrong of me to try and stop her, but you know how afraid I was that she might force me to go back to England.'

'As if I would've let that happen! Now you must stop worrying. I assure you Mordec hasn't the least suspicion that you had anything to do with it. He thinks he's got all the answers. He'll tell Lily that I tried to stop her, but only when they're far away from here. He gave me his word and I trust him. Brimful of Viking honour is Mordec. And Gus. Which is good, of course, for the future of the

Vikings. Honour must keep them going until they can be civilized.'

'Rory?'

'Yes, darling?'

'Do you think Lily likes Gus very much?'

'Gus? I don't know. I thought she liked Mordec.'

'Mordec? Oh yes she *likes* Mordec but I think she might one day *fall in love* with Gus. I wonder what that will mean for my queendom.'

'Your queendom? This is something new! When were you ever bothered about your queendom? You're talking nonsense.'

'Rory! How can you speak to me like that?'

'I'm sorry.'

'I forgive you. And let's not talk about it any more.'

end and beginning

In the autumn of that year the Army of the Redeemed marched through Germany and northern Italy attacking pagan and other non-Christian settlements, killing and looting, although it was said that the Church and the Black Monks—who had inspired, trained and armed them—had given no such orders. In some settlements the people were murdered to the last man, woman and child.

But then the Army began to encounter clusters of Vikings who fought them off, pursued them, and slaughtered them with as little mercy as they themselves had shown, so the holy warriors became wary of Vikings and avoided the places where they lived or regularly traded.

In the region of the Lombards, where some of the people were Christians and some not, slaughter and damage were piecemeal. The town of Gaudium Brevis had been marked down as a special target. The Army set off to wipe it from the face of the earth but on the way the leaders learnt that a Viking garrison had been established there, and they passed it by.

As with drums and hymns they streamed along the road, the citizens of Brevis watched from their watchtower, listened from their houses. Well-practiced swordsmen, men of the town, waited behind the closed gates under Viking command, and along the top of the walls Viking archers stood with bows at the ready.

Among them strange new weapons were mounted which could shoot as many as fifty rocks when a single taut rope was severed with an axe-blow. But not a blow was needed to be struck, not an arrow shot, not one volley of rocks flung against the enemy. The town survived and prospered.

On the very day the holy warriors went by Gaudium Brevis, the boy Pope was murdered by the Emperor's soldiers in Rome. His elephant was put up for sale. A Lombard bought it and presented it to a citizen of Nebulo so that he could go out riding in the summer high above the flowers whose scent and pollen troubled his sensitive nose.

While all this was happening, Mordec, Gus and Lily were travelling to England. It was to prove a perilous voyage.

www.ingramcontent.com/pod-product-compliance
Lightning Source LLC
Chambersburg PA
CBHW050139110726
47898CB00008B/2593